Books by Mark Gengler

Noah Thorne

Thanks a Lot, God!

Thanks A Lot, God

Mark Gengler

CM Christopher Matthews Publishing

Thanks a Lot, God!

Editor: Jeremy Soldevilla
Cover design: MJC Imageworks
Typeface: Georgia

ISBN 978-1-945146-38-1
ebook ISBN 978-1-945146-39-8

Published by

Christopher Matthews Publishing
www.christophermatthewspub.com
Boston

This book is dedicated to any service person
who has ever gotten a 'dear John' letter.

Also to the wonderful women who give their lives and
futures to the service of their faith.

Chapter One

MY NAME IS Hollis Olmstead. I was born in 1939 and raised on a small farm in northern Wisconsin. Dad was a reluctant farmer. His father wanted him to farm, so he did. Because his heart wasn't in it, he was not a very good farmer. The family got by, barely.

We got electricity in the house when I was five. We got a telephone when I was seven. The radio came somewhere in between. The television arrived just before I turned eleven. Hard times showed up before I was born and didn't leave until Dad sold the farm and we moved into town.

Mom was a reluctant mother. She had two children because she was Catholic. She was raised to believe that a child's behavior was formed using either a large wooden spoon or a stool in the corner. I chose the stool whenever I could. One day when I was six, I asked Mom, "Do frogs fart?" I had heard my dad and uncles use the word "fart" many times and thought it was acceptable. In keeping with the Catholic religion at the time, it was not acceptable for six-year-old boys. I took my old friend, the stool, and we retired to the corner. As I sat there asking God to forgive me for my foul mouth, I wondered, at what age is it okay to be a foul-mouthed sinner? Why do some women have moustaches? Does Santa Claus have an outhouse at the North Pole? Why can't birds fly backwards? These were all things nobody ever talked about, so asking questions would be a waste of time. I decided to pay more attention to the people around me.

The old saying 'be careful what you wish for . . .' is so true. I wished for answers to my questions, and what I got were more questions.

I began to observe closely the grown-ups I came in contact with. My grade school teacher was an interesting study of adult behavior. She did not really like children but taught them because it was her source of income. Most of their personal habits disgusted her. She didn't have to say a word. It showed in her face and in her actions. We tolerated each other for 8 years, and I never knew her first name. She never married and shaved her moustache once a week on Sunday night.

By force of will, I reluctantly refuse to disclose any of the observations I may have made of my uncles, aunts or cousins. I do this to honor the dead and avoid lawsuits from the living.

Being Catholic, I was able to observe several priests and nuns during my formative years. They proved to be a wealth of information. The only drawback was not being able to question them. My first lesson in religious instruction was to never question your religious instruction. There were so many things I wished to know that I could not ask. Does God wear bib overalls? Why do I have to tell a priest my sins if God already knows them? Do they have Friday fish-frys in heaven? Does the Pope go to confession? Do nuns take special classes on how to use a ruler? Who did Adam & Eve's children marry to have children? Any one of these questions would not have gotten me thrown out of the church, they would, however, have given me many happy hours in my favorite corner with my old friend, the stool.

CHAPTER TWO

MY VERY EARLY TEEN YEARS were a discovery period. I found that certain organs on my body served more than one purpose. My dad must have realized I had entered that stage of development that required 'the talk.' As he sweated, wrung his hands and refused to look at me, he explained about birds, bees, love, marriage and babies.

The word "sex" never came up, so I asked, "Is this where men and women have sex?" He turned pale and nodded his head. Remember when I told you I had been raised on a farm? The point being, if it is right there in front of you, pay attention!

I also began to notice the girls in school were developing shapes and curves that intrigued me. These were the same girls that six months ago were almost invisible. Now they were becoming desirable. I also noticed that boys my age were still mostly undesirable. We had pimples, no muscles to speak of, some skinny, some fat and some even uglier than me. We were a pathetic lot with bad breath and no vocal skills.

High school dances were supposed to be a fun time of getting to know the opposite sex. My first high school dance went like this. The girls who had developed were mobbed by the older boys. Those girls who had not begun to blossom formed a group against one wall of the auditorium. Against the opposite wall were the boys who hoped some girl would ask them to dance. This was my group. As I stood there scratching my armpit where the hair had just begun to grow, questions began to form in my mind. Why was I afraid to dance? If I asked, would I be rejected? Why do glasses make some girls attractive and others not? What would happen if I farted while dancing? Which undeveloped girl was the best looking? I waited for a slow song and made my move.

With my hands in my pockets, I calmly strolled over to the group of girls, settled on one about my height and squeaked out, "would you like to dance?" She nodded her head and held out her hand. I gently took it, and as our sweaty palms met, she looked directly at me and smiled. We moved around the floor in a I-don't-know-how-to-dance shuffle.

When the music ended, she said, "My name is Darla."

I told her mine and led her back to her group. Most of my questions had been answered in that encounter except one. The urge to pass gas had not arisen, and I complimented myself on my control.

The early teen years are a period of rejection. If you muster up the courage to ask a girl for a date, you will be rejected for many reasons. You have no car, no money, no social standing and no future in the eyes of the female gender. The following is a typical teen rejection:

"Hello; my name is Hollis."

"Get lost, Hollis."

"Thank you for a kind rejection."

With so much time on my hands, it was logical to explore the realm of questions again. Does Batman sleep hanging upside-down? Is there only one Easter Bunny, or does each state have its own bunny? Has daylight Savings time ever saved any daylight? Do Santa's reindeer poop on people's houses? Why is the ocean salty? The things that ran through my mind never actually scared me, but they did make me question my priorities.

Finally, to help out a friend, I agreed to go on a blind date. After his begging and pleading with me for 2.5 seconds, I said okay.

We were going to a drive-in movie. My friend had a car, money and a girlfriend named Wendy. Wendy had a girlfriend named Agnes who was desperate for a date. Agnes had a little less acne than I did and had developed a shape called "rotund." Her teeth were lovely thanks to the Dentyne gum she was chewing with vigor. She looked at me with a my-God-how-low-have-I-sunk look. We grunted hello at each other and sat at each end of the backseat of my friend's car.

My friend and Wendy became one in the front. The movie was *Godzilla,* and it was loud and not well-done. At the intermission, my friend and I went to the snack bar and each got a cheese pizza. When we got back in the car, I took a slice and handed the box to Agnes. That was the last I ever saw of it. I am not sure she ate the box, but I never saw it again.

After the movie, my friend dropped me off first, and that was the last I ever saw of him. I took heart in the fact that I had actually been on a date with a girl! No holding hands, no kissing, no cuddling, no touching of any kind. But it was a real date! I had broken the ice, and things would get better as I got older.

CHAPTER THREE

I TALKED MY OLDER BROTHER TIM into teaching me to drive. I got a temporary permit. I read the little booklet from cover to cover. I tested myself on what I had learned. I read the booklet again, and this time my brother tested me. Two days later, I got behind the wheel of my brother's car. By the end of the week, I was driving like an old pro.

I asked my dad to take me for my driving test. His answer intrigued me, and I spent three more days searching the sky for pigs with wings. After another week of groveling, Dad finally gave in and took me to the DMV for the test. The first time, I failed the parallel parking test. The second time, I actually passed and got my license!

* * *

In the summer of my seventeenth year, I was on my way to adulthood. All I needed was a job and a car. There was a canning factory in town that hired unsuspecting youths at minimum wage to process their vegetables into marketable wares. I worked on the line, putting cans in boxes. The heat and steam from the cookers made everything slippery, so we were told to bring gloves. Questions formed in my mind. Were they worried about the cans or my hands? How much did gloves cost? Were they too cheap to supply gloves? Was the Lone Ranger AWOL from his Ranger unit? What did training bras actually train breasts to do? I had a lot of time to think as I stood in one spot and filled boxes with cans.

My first paycheck was $62.00 for two weeks' work. I opened a savings account with $10.00. At this rate, I would own my first used-car at age 25. I felt it only right to give my mom money for room and board. Sleeping inside and eating at a table appealed to me. Some money was spent on entertainment. When you are sixteen, entertaining yourself alone can be fun if you can find the right books. I considered buying gloves for work, but the budget would not allow it, so I found a pair of Dad's old work gloves which worked fine.

* * *

There was a girl who lived two houses down from us. Her name was Beverly, and my brother Tim said she really liked boys. He had dated her a few times when no one else was available. I walked to her house and introduced myself. I learned she did like boys who owned cars. I told her I was working on getting one. She said, "come back when you have one."

Fortunately, I was a master at handling rejection and did not wish her any misfortune other than an incurable disease.

* * *

I graduated high school at age eighteen. The teaching staff was as surprised as I was. The whole thing was anticlimactic. I walked to the school one evening, put on a cap and gown, got a diploma, took off the cap and gown and went home. No muss, no fuss, no party and no gifts.

The next day, I was back to work at the canning factory. I had worked my way up from the boxing line to the loading dock. It was a 25-cent raise, and the hard work was beginning to give my body definition. The acne was gone, I had grown to 5 ft. 8 in., muscles were forming on my biceps, and both testicles had dropped. No hair on my chest yet, but there was still time.

There was a girl who worked in the office at the factory. Her name was Julia, and she was seventeen. I had said hello to her on occasion when I picked up my paycheck. She began to smile and say hello. She was kind of cute, wore her dark hair short and had enough figure to be called female. Her mother always picked her up after work in the family station wagon.

One day after work, I noticed she was walking home. It was in the same direction I was going, so I caught up to her and offered to walk her to her house. She agreed and told me their station wagon was in the garage getting new brakes. We had gone to the same high school but never met. I asked her if she would like to go on a date sometime, and she said she would ask her mother, but it probably would be okay. I told her I had no car, but we could walk to the movies or the drugstore.

Julia's mother met us at the door and invited me in. We sat in the living room, and I was grilled like a suspected criminal. Where do you live? Where does your father work? How much do you save from your income? Which church do you attend? Have you plans for your future? After a half-hour of this, I asked Julia's mother if it would be all right if I took Julia to a movie. She said she would drive us to the movie, see it with us and drive us home. Julia smiled and nodded her head as if this was perfectly fine with her. As I got up to leave, I said I would call to set up a date after I checked my busy schedule.

On my way home, I began to suspect that Julia's first kiss would be at the alter when she got married. I took the phone number she had given me and stuck it in the back of my wallet where it would never be in the way of any daily activities. I would see Julia from afar on occasion.

One day, as I picked up my check, she asked when I thought I would be able to take in a movie. I said I was saving up to splurge on a soda at the drugstore after the movie. She gave me that you-big-fat-liar look and officially ended our relationship.

One of the guys I worked with said he would double date if I would take his sister along. I demanded to see a picture before committing to anything. He showed me a picture of a skinny girl with two front teeth missing hugging a shaggy dog. I said his sister looked very friendly and asked who was the girl hugging her. He said it was an old picture and she was much better looking now. His suggestion was taking in a drive-in movie. I asked if his sister had ever eaten a pizza box. He said she liked pizza but had never seen her eat the box. I asked her name, and he said it was Miriam. I thought, *what the hell do I have to lose?* and agreed to go. I was to meet my first real girlfriend.

MIRIAM WAS ATTRACTIVE. She had long blonde hair she liked to wear in a ponytail. Her two front teeth had returned, and her hazel eyes had long lashes. Her figure was beyond the hopes of any eighteen-year-old boy. She was seventeen and stood 5ft. 6in..

My co-worker and his date picked me up, and as I got in the backseat of his car, Miriam said, "Hey, you're kind of cute."

I had suspected this for some time, but I was glad an attractive girl had noticed it.

We actually sat together in the middle of the backseat and talked! I asked about the picture of her and the dog. She laughed and told me her brother kept the picture because it had been his dog. She asked why I didn't have a girlfriend. I informed her that girls my age seldom dated boys my age who didn't have a car. I asked why a girl as cute as her didn't have a boyfriend. She told me she had just broken up with a boy whose idea of conversation was, "Let me see your tits."

I don't remember the movie. I remember the way the dim light flickered across her face as the film rolled on. At intermission, we all went to the food stand and got Cokes and hot dogs. No, she did not eat the wrapper. She held my hand loosely like a friend would. We all got back in the car and ate and drank, and she and I talked about everything. She wanted to know why boys did so many weird things. I asked the same questions of her about girls. Her brother turned around and asked us to be quiet so they could hear the speaker. We talked quietly through the rest of the movie. When I was dropped off in front of my house, she told me her phone number and said I better call within two days. To this day I still remember the number.

The next morning, I asked my dad again if I could borrow the car Friday night. I expected to be told I would again be on flying pig patrol, but Dad gave me a long look and said, "There better be a half-tank of gas when you get back."

I called Miriam and asked if she could go out Friday night. She checked with her mother and said, "I can go, but I have to be home by eleven, and my parents want to meet you first."

I was going on an actual date with a pretty girl, in a car! I almost peed my pants!

* * *

The rest of the summer passed in a blur of hazel eyes, laughter and endless conversations—mostly questions. Why do girls act like they don't like a boy if they really do? Why do boys think farts are funny? Why do parents tell kids they are not arguing when they really are? Do boys only think about sex and cars? Does Superman leave his wallet in his pants when he changes in the phone booth? If a doctor who thinks he is God gets sick, where does he go for a second opinion? Why do male world leaders wear make-up but female world leaders don't? Neither of us had many answers, but it didn't matter.

It was fun being together. Miriam asked me why I didn't stare at her bountiful breasts like other boys did. I replied that I would gladly pay more attention to her breasts if she wished, but I also enjoyed looking into her beautiful eyes. With an evil little smile, she gently took my hand and laid it atop her round right breast.

"That's because you didn't ask for it and you gave me the right answer to my question," she said softly. She took my hand away and kissed me.

CHAPTER FIVE

MIRIAM TURNED EIGHTEEN in October. Her parents gave her a small party at their home. She looked stunning in a new summer dress.

Suddenly, her mother gasped and rushed her into the house. She had noticed the same thing I did. When the sun hit the dress at just the right angle, it became almost transparent. She was wearing matching pink panties and bra. I silently cursed her mother for being observant, but then thought, *If I can see through her dress, so can everyone else*; and removed the curse.

Miriam came back out blushing and wearing jeans and a T-shirt. There was no beer, but there were plenty of rock & roll records to play on the small record player. There was cake and presents from family and girlfriends. I had gone all out and gotten her a huge wall poster of Elvis Presley, her favorite singer.

After the party, we played mini-golf, one of our favorite pastimes. I told her I was looking for a different job, one that had a real future. I thought I might use my savings and attend a trade school, but I hadn't decided what I wanted to do for a career. She told me her mother was teaching her to cook and bake, and soon I would be invited over for a meal she had cooked by herself. We were planning for our future together.

* * *

I turned nineteen in December. The canning factory had closed for the season, so I was working at a department store stocking shelves and delivering furniture. It paid 50 cents an hour more than the canning factory, and I got to drive the delivery truck. I had begun my journey to adulthood, and everything was going as Miriam, and I planned.

My parents liked Miriam and invited her over often. My dad marveled that such a smart, attractive girl was actually dating me. My mom told her all about my childhood, which embarrassed me to no end but seemed to delight Miriam. Her being Catholic also endeared her to my mother.

Christmas was a flurry of presents, parties and making plans for the coming new year. I was looking around for a good used-car but what I liked was out of my price range. The manager of the department store was impressed with the way I dealt with the customers I delivered furniture to. He said he was thinking of moving me to the sales department. I asked him how much that paid. He said I would work on commission. If I sold a lot of stuff. I would make a lot of money. Instantly I realized that if I didn't sell much. I wouldn't make much. Some men were born salesmen, I was a born laborer. I told him I would give it a great deal of thought and let him know. He frowned a little, nodded his head and walked away.

In February, my future took a turn for the worse. I got a letter from the department of the Army informing me I had been drafted! I would be reporting to Fort Knox, Kentucky, for basic training at the end of the month. I broke the news to Miriam, and the tears flowed freely. She cried a lot too. I questioned this detour on my life's journey, but there was really nothing I could do but go. I told the department store manager and showed him the letter. He shook my hand and wished me well. My dad told me to do my best and don't get VD. Mom sniffled as she laid out new plans for my room. My brother shook my hand and told me to send him a picture of me in my uniform. On our last night together, Miriam and I hugged and swore eternal love. We promised to write every week and send pictures of each other. The next morning, I boarded the train that would change my life.

CHAPTER SIX

THE TRAIN STOPPED at many small stations along the way to pick up other boys who had also been drafted. Some were hungover, some were still drunk, some were happy to be going and some, like me, were still pissed off at being torn from a happy situation and taken to who-knows-what. We all gradually separated into groups. The drinkers, the whiners, the I-wanna-go-homers and the rest of us. We told each other our names and where we were from. Some of the guys had long hair, and a few had moustaches.

We talked about our families and girlfriends and passed pictures around. Miriam got several whistles, and I felt very proud until one guy showed us a picture of his girl without a bra. I whistled at her. We discussed the fact that if you enlisted you served three years but if you were drafted you only had to serve two years. The entire trip took 18 hours, and soon we pulled into the station at Louisville, Kentucky.

"Get your ass off the train and get in the truck!" This was our first official order from the U.S. Army. Several hard-looking men wearing pressed uniforms herded us into a line of Army trucks for the 28-mile trip to Fort Knox. When I boarded the train at home, there was snow on the ground, and the temperature was 10 degrees. Here, the temperature felt about 60 degrees and no snow. I wasn't happy to be here, but at least it was warm. The trucks pulled into a parking area near some wooden buildings I would learn to call barracks.

We were ordered out of the trucks and told to line up in three rows and stand at attention. An older white sergeant and a younger Negro sergeant yelled, poked and prodded us into a semblance of recruits standing at attention. The white sergeant's name was Vance. The Negro sergeant's name was Green.

Sergeant Vance said, "When I call off your name, answer, 'here,' not 'yo,' not 'yes' but 'here.'"

His accent was thick, but if he talked slowly, I was sure I could understand him. I learned later he was from Missouri. After roll call, we were instructed to take our bags into the barracks and assemble outside again. We were then marched to the barbershop. I had always worn my hair short, so this was no big deal for me. For some others it was traumatic. After the haircut, we were marched to the uniform warehouse. We lined up, got a duffle-bag, caught the clothing thrown at us and stuffed it all into the bag. No one asked what size you were or if you liked boxers or briefs. We were given four of everything. Shirts, pants, T-shirts, boxers and pairs of socks. We were measured for shoes and boots, one pair of each. Overcoat, gloves and liners, helmet and liner and woolen muffler. All this wealth was then taken back to the barracks, and we were marched to lunch. I expected at some point to be marched to the latrine but some things we were expected to do ourselves.

The next morning, we fell out for roll call. We were missing two people. We learned later they had decided to walk into Louisville and take the train home. It was wise to leave in the dark but not wise to take the wrong road and end up at the tank training ground. I don't know what happened to them, but they did not rejoin us.

We were marched to breakfast and then to a long building where we got medical exams and shots. We then filed into another building where we were seated and lectured on what was expected of us during our training. We were shown a film about the terrors of VD. There was no training program on how to prevent it, and I wondered why we were shown this now. For the next six weeks, we were not allowed off the base, so this must have been classed as entertainment.

The basic training routine was a mixture of new fun things like learning the workings of the M-1 Garand rifle, and new agonizing things like the ten-mile hike with full pack and the wonderful rifle. In between, we learned how to defend ourselves against a charging bayonet and how to survive a gas attack.

I wrote Miriam a letter every week telling her what we were doing. She wrote back telling me about new rock & roll songs and new movies. She sent a picture of her and her brother. He was teaching her to drive his car. I missed her terribly and longed to be home.

Finally, after six weeks that seemed like six months, we had a big parade, given new orders and two weeks leave. We were driven back into Louisville to the train station and headed home.

* * *

We had a great reunion. My family and Miriam met me at the train station. My brother shook my hand awkwardly like I was still his little brother but different. Dad patted my shoulder and commented on how I had filled out. I had gained some weight and some muscle. Mom hugged me briefly and kissed my cheek. Miriam did the same.

Mom had a big meal planned for that night, and Miriam helped her cook. I sat in the living room and told my dad and brother all about Army life. Later, I drove Miriam home, and we planned to go to a movie the next night. She told me she had not even seen another boy since I left. Apparently, she had been reading the Bible a lot and had been going to church twice a week. She said God had helped her through our separation, and she was learning a lot from the Bible. To me, this was wonderful news! She was not interested in other boys, only me. Thanks a lot, God!

Tim took me out one night with some of his friends. They wanted to impress me with the amount of beer they could drink. I got a little drunk, and the rest of the guys made me look cold sober. My brother passed out in his car about midnight. Another I found in the restroom donating his supper to the toilet. The third one I never found, so I took the other two home and left them sleeping in the car overnight while I went to bed.

Most of my time was spent with Miriam, and we enjoyed being together. I even attended Mass on Wednesday night with her. She could recite verses of the Bible I had never heard of. She said it gave her a wonderful, peaceful feeling. She even cooked supper at her parents' house for us one night. It was the best meatloaf I ever tasted. She had me tell her parents all about the Army and what I had learned.

All too soon, it was time to leave for my regular posting at Fort Stewart, Georgia. Miriam drove me to the train station, and we kissed a long goodbye. We promised to write every week again until I could get another leave. As I waved to her from the window of the train, I could not even imagine it would be years before I saw her again.

* * *

I was now officially a member of the 3rd Infantry Division. I took my Advanced Infantry training and was assigned to the motor pool. I was surprised to learn that only two in ten draftees and drivers licenses. I was trained in the workings of the M38A1 Willys Jeep and was assigned to a general transportation unit. We transported everyone except generals. Figure that one out! Normally, if an officer above the rank of lieutenant needed transport, one of us would pick him up and be his driver for the day.

I was also authorized to drive the 2.5-ton truck and often did. I liked the duty and soon was promoted from Private First Class to Specialist E-4. I was sending home savings bonds that I could cash in later with interest.

The summer was hot and humid with occasional rain that turned the Georgia clay to a bright red muck that was hell to drive through. Without 4-wheel drive, it would have been impossible.

Miriam and I wrote every week as promised. I would tell her about the officers I drove around, and she would tell me about new Bible verses. I told her how much I missed her, and she told me about working as a layperson at the church.

I waited for mail-call every day. Sometimes my mom would write with home news. I never got a letter from my brother, but then, I never expected to. The week before I had written Miriam that I had been in the Army for nine months now and was soon due for a leave. I told her I had something really important to ask her. I had not yet talked to her about getting married, but I figured now was as good a time as any. I got back a four-page letter. Miriam said she loved me more than anyone in her life except God and that she was leaving home to begin postulant training and would be gone for a year. She hoped I would understand. She said she had gotten the call to dedicate her life to God and would become a nun!

What the hell?!

This was not happening to me! While I was off serving my country, God had stolen my girlfriend! I was so stunned I just sat there right through chow time. The letter slowly slipped from my hands and drifted to the floor. I knew a few guys who had gotten a 'Dear John' letter, but this was ridiculous! How dare God take my Miriam! How dare Miriam leave me for him! I reported back for duty in a fog. Luckily, I was not driving anyone that day. I was washing down vehicles. When the fog wore off, it was replaced by anger and resentment. I would show her what I thought of her calling!

I tore each page of Miriam's letter into four pieces. I put all the pieces into a large envelope and mailed it back to her. Within days, I got another letter from her on which I wrote, 'return to sender,' and sent it back. After the fourth letter, she finally stopped writing.

Then I got a letter from my mom asking me to please get in touch with Miriam, and why was I breaking her heart? Her heart? What about my heart?! I wrote back to Mom and told her she was never to write to me about that girl ever again! If she did, I would send the letter back. Mom never mentioned Miriam again.

I did not take a leave that year. I took the pay instead and bought more savings bonds. I was forming a new plan for my life. My journey would take me down a very different road. I did take a three-day pass and took the bus to Hinesville, Georgia. I vaguely recall getting drunk and donating my virginity to a chunky blonde bar girl with bad breath. Then I got drunk again. When I sobered up, I felt like a hungover fool. I caught the bus back to the base and went back to work.

* * *

I began to realize that this was the first real crisis that I had happen in my short life and I had probably handled it badly. I thought about possibly getting in touch with Miriam and telling her how I felt but eventually decided against it. There was still a spark of feeling for her and I didn't want to confuse her or deter her from following what she felt was her life's journey. It took months for the anger and hurt to go into hiding in a small secret corner of my heart. It would not leave, but it would not torment me either.

Thanks a lot, God!

CHAPTER SEVEN

M Y TIME WITH UNCLE SAM was almost up. I was now a Specialist-5. The savings bonds had been going home for two years, and I had almost $500 dollars saved up. I was asked to re-enlist but politely told the recruiter what to do with his offer. I had not wanted to be here in the first place, why would I want to continue to stay? Recruiters are a little different from regular Army. They take rejection rather well.

It took about three weeks to clear everything up. I had to turn in everything except the uniform I would wear home. My records had to be cleared, and a medical exam was given to prove I was in better shape than when I had entered, which I was. I stood 5 ft. 10 in. tall and weighed 185 pounds. In between bouts of activity, I was allowed free time, which the Army generously filled with KP duty. Then, one day, I was free to go. I rode the bus into Hinesville and bought a train ticket home.

I loved riding the train. It was a way to see a lot of the country and travel at the same time. It also gave me time to think. My plan was to buy a car and travel across America. I thought it wise to see what I had been defending for two years. My life was now mine to do with as I wished. When I ran low on money, I would stop and work for a while. A friend from the motor pool at Fort Stewart had told me he was from a small town in Nebraska that had a construction company that was always hiring people. This seemed a good place to start.

* * *

My brother met me at the train station. He looked older and seemed to be much more calmed down. On the ride home, he told me he and his girlfriend were getting married in June. He asked me to be his best man. This meant putting my plans on hold three months at least, but I told him I would be honored.

Her name was Connie, and I would meet her later at dinner. I knew Tim was going to want to tell me about Miriam so I said, "We can talk about everything except Miriam." This seemed to put a damper on the conversation, and we were pretty quiet until we got home.

Dad was at work, but Mom was home and gave me a hug and a kiss on the cheek. I gave her the same instructions I had given my brother, and she just nodded her head. I dumped my bag in my old room and asked Mom where were all the savings bonds I had sent home.

She went to the desk and took out a packet of envelopes in a rubber band.

It was Friday afternoon, and I asked my brother if we could go look at some cars for sale tomorrow. He said he already had a few picked out I might like.

The next day, I cashed in my bonds and drew my savings out of the bank. The savings plus interest plus the bonds gave me a grand total of $607.00. I found a five-year-old Ford Fairlane in good shape for $425. It ran great but needed new tires, which cost me $75. This left me $100 to begin my journey, but I had to wait three months to go, which would eat into my capital. I headed to the department store where I used to work to see if my old job was available. There was a new manager who was a veteran of the Korean War, and he hired me that day at $5 an hour. I told him my plan to travel, and he said, "Don't worry about it, just do a good job while you're here."

* * *

The wedding happened on a sunny June afternoon. The bride was beautiful, and my brother was nervous. As they walked down the aisle on the way out of church, I felt the pull of the road calling me to begin my journey. I was already packed and left the next morning after promising Mom I would write or call to let her know where I was. I had saved a little over $300 working at the store and gas was cheap. I headed for Nebraska.

Chapter Eight

THE FEELING OF HAVING total control over your future is difficult to put into words. It a lot of day-to-day freedom mixed with a little responsibility and a dash of fear you may do something really stupid.

As I motored along, I watched the speedometer and kept to the speed limit. I had left home at 5 a.m., just as the sun showed its first rays. I stopped once at a truck stop for gas and food. Truck stops are supposed to have the best food, but this one never got the word. I ate about half the meatloaf and some of the lumpy mashed potatoes and none of the peas.

The waitress asked, "What's the matter, not hungry this morning?"

I said I was hungry but would have preferred food instead of what I got. She gave me that 'I'll-bet-you're-a-lousy-tipper' look. She was wrong. I tipped according to the food and the service. Having received neither, I left no tip at all.

I crossed the Nebraska state line around noon and stopped to check my map. The town I was looking for was about an hour away. When I got there, I stopped for gas again and asked the pump jockey where was a good place to eat.

He smiled and said, "Try Kansas."

I admire a sense of humor but dislike smartasses. As I drove through town, I marveled how all small towns looked alike. Same layout, same businesses and the same distrust of strangers.

I pulled up and parked in front of a a place with a faded sign that said 'Mom's Diner.' It was mid-afternoon, and the place was very clean but almost empty. I sat at the counter, and the waitress handed me a menu. Her name tag said 'Helen.' She was probably in her late 40's but had a nice smile. I ordered a coke and a hamburger with fries. As she wiped down the counter, she asked if I were new in town or just passing through. I told her I was looking for work and asked if she knew about the construction company I was looking for and where it was located. Giving me a frown, she told me I would not like working there. It was a hell-hole and the guy running it was a crook. As I pondered this information, she asked if I knew anything about building houses. I said no, but I was a fast learner.

"My brother is building some houses in a new development area west of town. If you think you can do the work, I'll call him and see if he needs anyone."

I gave her my best smile, said thank you and dug into the French fries. She came back in a minute and handed me a slip of paper with a name and address on it and gave me directions. This was my kind of waitress! I left her a ten-dollar bill for a $4.50 tab and got back in the car.

The guy's name was Pete, and he had fired someone that morning. Pete had two rules to follow. He wanted a day's work for a day's pay. The first time you were late under 15 minutes you got a warning. The next time you got fired.

"Do you know how to mix mud?" he asked me.

"Show me what it is, and I will mix all you need," I answered.

He smiled and said, "You will start work at 7 a.m. and work till 4 p.m. Monday through Friday. I will start you at eight dollars an hour, and you will earn every penny. Today is Thursday, so you don't get paid till next Friday. Report to Joe, the foreman, and he will show you all about mud."

I learned 'mud' is the mortar used to hold bricks or cement blocks together. Joe gave me the lecture on mixing 'mud.'

"To mix it in the cement mixer, you pour in a bag of cement, add four heaping shovels of sand and a half bucket of water. When the mix is ready, tip the mixer and fill the mud buckets. Carry them to the guys putting up the basement walls. Then go back and start all over again."

Whoever designed this system must have been an Army veteran.

I found a tourist court on the highway that rented me a cabin with bath for $25 a week. The place was clean, and the bed was comfortable. I paid for two weeks, laid my bag on the bed and went back into town to eat at Mom's Diner. Helen was off-duty, but a pretty freckled-faced redhead with a great figure waited on me. Her name tag said 'Sally,' and she had a smile that lit up her face and made her green eyes sparkle. I asked her what was good to eat.

"Try the fried chicken, it's really good," she said.

She was right. It came with seasoned potato wedges and green beans, and it was delicious. As I ate, I added up my good fortune—a decent job, a place to stay and a good place to eat. God and I were not really on speaking terms yet, so I didn't bother to thank him.

Mixing mud isn't exactly what you could call fun or challenging, but there was a certain sense of doing it right every time that appealed to me. The guys laying the blocks were happy the mud was there when they needed it, and the foreman was happy I showed up every morning and put in a good day's work. I was getting tanned and putting on some muscle where it was needed.

On Saturday nights, I took in a movie and dropped in to the local bar for a few beers and maybe a game of pool.

On Sunday, I just slept until noon, called Mom to let her know everything was going really well, and sometimes took an afternoon drive to see the sights. I was getting to be good friends with the waitress, Sally, and we compared notes on our home towns. She was engaged to be married to Andrew, the assistant manager of the hardware store.

It had been about a month, and things were falling into a routine—show up at seven, mix mud, break for lunch, mix more mud, go home at four. Then, one Monday morning, Pete stopped me as I was about to dump my first bag of cement into the mixer.

"Can you drive a truck?" he asked me.

I told him I had driven the Army deuce-and-a-half quite a bit.

"The company that delivers my lumber and roofing supplies has me at the bottom of their delivery list. Over the weekend I bought a two-ton flatbed truck. This way I can get my supplies as I need them." Pointing his finger at me, he continued, "If you think you can handle the job you get a dollar an hour raise."

I gave him my best smile and said, "Show me your truck and tell me where the lumber company is."

Pete led me around the side of the house trailer he used for an office, and there was a brown Chevy flatbed truck.

"Who is going to mix your mud?" I asked.

"I've some college kid coming who I hope will do as good a job as you did," he said. Pete handed me a list of what he needed and gave me directions.

I didn't expect it to be an easy job and I was right. The loading was done with a forklift, and Pete had a Bobcat to help unload. The hard part was getting the lumber company to get the order right. The first order, the company tried to short-change me on roof-struts and three rolls of tar-paper. I showed the guys Pete's list and said I would wait until I had the full load. The second time, they 'forgot' two cases of nails and a half-dozen bundles of shingles. After that, things ran a little smoother. In between loads, I was a 'gofer.' I carried bundles of shingles up the ladder to the roofers and hauled lumber inside half-completed shells for the carpenters. Overall, it beat mixing mud.

The Fourth of July fell on a Saturday. When I picked up my paycheck Friday afternoon, Pete said, "I'm having a cook-out at my house tomorrow about noon, I expect you to be there."

With my check was a slip of paper with directions to Pete's house. I drove to Mom's Diner, parked and stepped into the cool air-conditioning. Sally was behind the counter making iced tea and talking to another girl seated there. This girl also had red hair, but it was a darker color and fell in waves around her shoulders. Her figure was slender but filled out in all the right places. Her eyes were a soft green with long lashes. Whatever they were feeding the girls in Nebraska, it was working!

Sally said, "This is my sister Tina. I was telling her about you, and she wanted to meet you."

Tina was nineteen and home from college for the summer. We talked and drank iced tea for about an hour.

Finally, I said, "My boss is having a Fourth of July party at his house tomorrow afternoon, would you like to go?"

With a big smile, she said, "I would love to go. Can you pick me up about noon?"

Behind the counter, Sally laughed and said, "You be nice to him Tina; he is a friend of mine."

Tina winked at me and said to Sally, "Being nice is for little girls; I'm a big girl now."

I had to sit and drink iced tea for a few more minutes because if I stood up, Tina could have measured how much I was attracted to her.

The party at Pete's was just getting started when we arrived. One of the first people I saw was Helen, the waitress who got me my job. She introduced me to her husband Brad and asked how the job was going. I told her I was driving the delivery truck now.

"Pete would never have gotten that truck until you showed up," she said. "He was dead set against it until he found someone he could trust to handle the job."

She knew Tina and gave her a motherly hug, saying, "I should have known you two would hook up, you're both free spirits."

Pete strolled over and handed Tina and me a cold bottle of beer.

"I hope you don't mind that I brought a date," I said.

Pete laughed and said, "You took your time finding a girlfriend, but you show good taste. Food will be ready in about an hour."

Being a hometown girl, Tina knew most of the people there. She introduced me around, and we had a good time. We had burgers, hot dogs, cole slaw, potato salad, macaroni salad and about four different kinds of chips.

After about two hours and two beers, Tina suggested we take a drive. We left the happy gathering and got in the car.

"Let's drive down by the river and talk," she said. "We haven't really had a chance to get to know each other yet."

There was a small county park with a picnic table facing the river. As we sat down, she said, "Tell me about you and why are you here."

I told her about everything except Miriam and said when fall came I was probably moving on, maybe to Texas for the winter. Then I asked her about her life.

Tina liked writing. It began in high school when she was asked to work on the school paper. After graduating, she applied to The University of Nebraska at Lincoln. She was taking journalism as a major and worked at the paper here in town during the summer. It was a weekly paper, and she was doing human interest stories.

"A gorgeous girl like you should have guys lined up to date her," I said.

"I have a long-range plan for my future," she said, "and all the boys here in town are looking for stay-at-home wives. That's not me." She said when she graduated college she planned to work for one of the big papers, hopefully, New York, Chicago or Los Angeles.

"I like boys, and I enjoy sex, but I'm not looking for any permanent attachment right now," she added.

I suggested we get a six-pack of beer and go back to my place.

"Maybe you should stop by the drugstore and get a package of condoms—just in case," she said with a wink.

I got a box of condoms, just in case.

We both agreed it was the best Fourth of July we ever had. We talked, had a beer, had sex and then talked some more. By the time the sun was going down, we both decided we were ravenously hungry. We showered, got dressed and drove to the diner.

Hamburgers and onion rings disappeared as fast as the Cokes did. I took her home, and we made a date for Monday night to see a new movie in town. I wasn't in love, but I certainly was happy.

The work days were more pleasant, and the nights we were together were the best I had ever known. We kept telling each other it was okay to see other people, but we never did. We bowled, took in movies, went on picnics and once double-dated with her sister Sally and Andrew. We looked at maps of Texas trying to find the perfect small town for me this winter.

All too soon it was Labor Day, and Tina was packed and ready to go back to college. We both tried not to be sad, but we were. We promised to write and maybe see each other in the spring. Then she was gone, and I was lonely for her company.

* * *

I told Pete I was getting ready to move on. He asked where to, and I told him probably Texas.

He got a big smile on his face and said, "My first foreman was a guy named Frank. He now has his own construction company based in a small town not far from Lubbock, Texas. If you promise to come back here by the first of April, I'll give him a call and set you up for the winter."

We shook hands on it, and I left to pick up a load of material.

I stayed on the job until the first of October. I had been making good money working for Pete and decided to trade in the Fairlane for a pickup truck. I found a five-year-old Ford F-150 that didn't need anything except me in the driver's seat.

On my last Friday, Pete called me into his office at noon and handed me my paycheck.

"I called Frank, and he said he would give you a few days to settle in but needed you to start as soon as possible. I want you to take the rest of the day off. Stop by the diner and say goodbye to Helen. If you don't, she will kick my ass for a week."

I got in my new truck and drove to Mom's Diner. Helen and Sally were both there and treated me to a double burger & fries lunch. Eventually, they got around to the reason they wanted me to drop by. Tina and I had been writing, and her letters were short and light-hearted. She wrote mostly about the college and her courses she was taking. What I didn't know was she had been calling Sally and Helen asking if I was doing all right and was I seeing anybody else.

"She misses you terribly but refuses to admit it. How do you feel about her?" asked Sally.

I thought a minute and decided to tell them the truth. "I love her, but if I had told her, it would have scared her away. I want her to follow her dream, but I don't want to let her go."

Sally had tears in her eyes and Helen was nodding her head.

"You are doing exactly the right thing," said Helen, "Let her do what she needs to do but don't lose touch. She will graduate in June. Are you planning on coming back this way?"

I told her the deal I had with Pete to be back in April. We hugged, and I left to pick up my things at the tourist cabin. I told the owner I would be back in April and he said next year he would give me a special summer rate. We shook hands, and once again, I was a free man on the open road.

CHAPTER NINE

TEXAS WAS HOT and dusty. The lifestyle there was like a slow motion version of Nebraska. Nobody hurried, nobody ran anywhere. They walked slow, talked slow and took their time at everything. It took a while, but when I got used to it, I liked it.

I checked into a motel when I got to town, then drove to Frank's construction site. Frank's operation was different from Pete's. Frank was building two-story apartment buildings. He didn't mix mud, he had it delivered.

"I've got all the carpenters and masons I need," he told me. "What I don't have is a way to organize the deliveries with the workers. Pete said you were good at getting things done. Show me you can do it, and I'll start you at ten dollars an hour."

I got a list from Frank of all the companies he did business with. Then I went through the yellow pages of the local phone book and wrote down every lumber company, cement contractor, window and door company and plumbing contractor I could find. It took two weeks, but in the end, I had worked out a deal with each one.

After I switched to another lumber company, the rest fell into line. I visited each business and worked out new rates for better service. Frank not only paid the ten dollars an hour, in my first check was a $100 bonus.

I started each day at seven checking the deliveries with the orders. I had the lumber moved to a more efficient site and assigned the workers a new parking area to allow the delivery trucks better access. Any plumber or electrician who failed to show without calling in was replaced. Building inspectors now had to check in at the office before going on-site.

Frank spent his time on the phone in the trailer office, and I spent my time on-site making sure the guys had what they needed. Only one worker objected to the new way of doing business. I told him to talk to Frank. The next day he was gone.

I sent Tina a picture of me and my new truck in front of the building we were working on. She sent me a picture of her in front of the Lincoln College sign.

Thanksgiving came and went. The job kept me busy, but the weekends were long and lonely. I sometimes stopped on Friday night and had a few beers with the crew, maybe shot some pool.

One Sunday, for no good reason, I went to church. I was not angry with God anymore. After meeting Tina, I realized each life has a path to follow, and each of us must follow our heart to make a successful journey. Deep down I wished for the opportunity to tell Miriam that I was sorry I had acted like a fool over her decision. Maybe way down the road, I would get the chance. I guess that's why I went to church—to ask God for the hope that our paths would someday meet again.

On December 15th, Frank told me he was shutting down for the holidays until January 5th. I knew Tina would be home for Christmas break and decided it was time for a visit.

I drove out of Lubbock on a Saturday afternoon, and by Sunday morning, crossed the Nebraska state line.

About ten in the morning, I pulled into the driveway at Pete's house and knocked on the door. He opened it, smiled and shook my hand. He invited me in for coffee and called his wife.

"Brenda, we have company. Come see the pilgrim."

She walked in, threw her hands in the air and gave me a hug.

"Did you check in any place to stay yet?" Pete asked.

I told him I had just driven in and stopped here first.

"You'll stay here. I've been fixing up the basement as a spare room. You have your own bathroom and your own entrance off the kitchen."

I told him I was hoping to run into Tina.

"That's why you will need your own entrance," he said with a smile.

I put my bag in the spare room, and Pete and I drove to the diner.

It wasn't like being home, it was better. Pete asked all about working with Frank, and I told him what I had been doing.

Pete laughed and said, "I used to owe Frank a favor, now he owes me one."

He asked if I still planned on coming back in April.

I said, "Once I give my word that's it. Besides, I miss this town. I might settle here some day."

I noticed the town was growing up out along the highway. Pete said he had a contract to build in a new subdivision to the west. He had hired a second foreman so he could work in two different areas at once.

"When you get back, you will have to do for me what you did for Frank," he said.

Nobody was expecting me when we walked in. Helen gave a squeal and ran around the counter to give me a hug.

"Welcome home, stranger," she said with a laugh. "Sit down, and I will get you both some coffee."

I asked if Tina had made it home for Christmas.

With a sad smile, Helen said, "Tina is here, and she has been moping around like someone stole her pet puppy." Then she winked at me and whispered, "I am going to call Sally and have her bring Tina along when she comes to work at three. I'll tell her I have a Christmas present for her."

I looked at the clock, and it was just after two.

"You should have just enough time to drive me home and get back here at three," Pete said.

I thanked Helen, and we left.

I got back to the diner at five minutes to three. I looked in the door and saw Sally behind the counter tying on her white apron. Helen was putting on her coat and watching the door. She saw me and motioned me in with her hand.

Sally saw me and her hands flew to her mouth and her eyes got big. Helen made a shushing gesture with her finger to her lips.

Very off-handedly she said, "Oh, by the way, Tina, I almost forgot to give you your present."

Tina was sitting in a booth with her head down over a cup of hot chocolate. She raised her head, and I said, "Hi, gorgeous. Got room in that booth for an old friend?"

Her eyes got big, and she stood up slowly and put her hand to her mouth. She walked across the diner and slowly put her arms around me and hugged me so hard it was difficult to breathe. Her head was buried in my chest, and I could feel my T-shirt soaking up a warm wetness. When she raised her head, and I kissed her, she kept her eyes closed. I looked over at Sally and Helen who both had big smiles and tears in their eyes.

Helen patted Tina on the back and said, "Merry Christmas, hon," and left.

Sally came around the counter saying, "Okay, break it up for a minute so I can get my hug."

Tina finally let go, and I gave Sally a brief hug.

Tina led me over to her booth saying, "Don't you dare say a word about me crying. I'm just so glad to see you. I thought I would be spending Christmas alone and for the first time, I didn't like it one bit. I missed you every day, and it is scaring the hell out of me!"

I took both her hands in mine and said, "Neither one of us is ready to change dreams or goals at this point. I have plans too. I want both of us to achieve our future plans without giving up anything. But that doesn't mean I'm ready to end our relationship. I want it to grow and see where it leads us. Right now, right here, I am happy just to be with you and know that you feel the same."

"I thought this was going to be my worst Christmas ever," she said with a smile. "Now I think it could be the best one ever."

It was the best Christmas *I* ever experienced. Everybody wanted to host a party, and Tina and I were invited to all of them. I had been adopted by a town! I gave Tina a locket with our names on it. She loved it. She gave me a wrist watch. On the back was engraved, 'Taking our time.' It was perfect.

Then, one day, it was time to say goodbye until April. This parting was different. It held promise and hope.

CHAPTER TEN

FRANK WAS WAITING FOR ME when I got back in January.

"Three of my builders quit over the holidays. Where can I find good help right now?" he wanted to know.

"Give me two hours, and I will bring you the best workers you ever had," I told him.

I left and drove to the Veteran's Affairs office in town. The guy there looked at me like I had dropped from heaven.

"I've got four guys just out of the Marines looking for work," he said. "Can you hire them all?"

I gave him the address of Frank's construction site and told him to have all four report there as soon as possible.

When I got back to Frank's office, three of them were there, and the fourth pulled in behind me. I told the guys to wait outside, and I went in.

I told Frank I had four guys ready to work.

"But I only need three," he said.

I reminded him that I would be leaving in April. I said I would train one of them to take my place, but it would take at least three months.

Nodding his head, Frank said, "I was going to talk my head off to get you to stay, but if your mind is made up I guess I'll hire them all. I sure hope you know what you're doing."

I said, "They are all Marine veterans, Frank. They are used to showing up on time and following orders. What more could you ask for?"

The new guys fit right in, and things ran smoothly. The guy I picked to replace me was named George, he was a six-year veteran of the Corps and needed very little training. He caught on to the routine and even made a few suggestions that worked out great. He had a wife and two kids, and this was his meal ticket to the good life.

Frank was happy. The new guys were working out better than the ones who quit. He did try his best to keep me there. He promised a raise, a company truck and season tickets to the Dallas Cowboys games.

I told him thanks, it sounded great, but I had made Pete a promise I could not break.

"Dammit, now I owe *him* a favor, and he won't let me forget it," he said with a scowl.

The days dragged by, and I tried to fill in my free time with planning what I wanted to do for my life's work. I was in the right field, but I needed something specific to interest me.

After calling Mom one Sunday morning, I decided to go to Mass again. The weather was beautiful, and the church was only about half full. I sat in the back and took in the sounds and sights of a worship service. Somewhere in the middle of the sermon, the priest mentioned something about the beauty of a spring day.

After Mass was over, I took a drive out to the houses we were working on and parked across the street to get a full view of the scene. It looked like what it was—a work in progress. The houses were all built from a contractor's point of view. They all looked the same. I got back in the truck and drove to the older section of town. Here were homes with their own identity, their own personality. Many of them were brick or fieldstone. This was what I wanted for a house. I liked the look of a home that told you it was patiently put together by masters of their trade. I wanted to learn to build with this kind of material. I would talk to Pete when I got back and work out a plan to learn this trade.

* * *

The last Friday in March was my last day of work in Texas. I walked the site with a few inspectors and checked the deliveries as they arrived. At noon, George asked if he could borrow my truck for an errand he needed to run. I handed him the keys and thought no more about it.

After lunch, Frank called me into the office and went over the duties George would be taking on. About two o'clock, George drove back onto the site, parked my truck in front of the trailer and got out with a big grin on his face. Then I noticed a few things had been done to my old F-150. It was sparkling clean and shiny as a new dime.

Frank came out of his office, patted me on the back and said, "We took a few liberties with your truck. You got an oil change, lube job, wash & wax and new tires. If you think I am still trying to get you to change your mind and stay, you're right."

I shook his hand and said, "If I ever get tired of Nebraska this will be my next stop."

Frank laughed and said, "Hit the road, cowboy; go see that girl you're always talking about and thank Pete for me."

I said goodbye to the crew, and as I was about to climb into the cab, George and the three other Marines handed me a small package. I opened it and took out a St. Christopher medal.

"It to hang on your rear-view mirror and keep you safe as you travel. We won't forget what you did for us."

I thanked them and hung the medal on the mirror. I drove to the motel and packed my stuff. It was time to go home.

Chapter Eleven

I T'S ABOUT A TWELVE-HOUR DRIVE from Texas to Nebraska. I stopped for gas and a burger at a truck stop. The weather was warm, and spring was in full bloom. I was looking forward to maybe finding an apartment this time. I was not yet ready to go permanent with a house but needed something more than a tourist cabin.

The miles flew by as I drove with my window open and the radio turned up. It did not feel strange to call Nebraska home. That's where I felt like I belonged. I thought back on my plan to crisscross America and chuckled at the fact that I had never made it to the Colorado state line. My journey was not proceeding according to my plan but seemed to have its own plan. I wondered if God was involved in why and where I was traveling this particular path in my life.

I did resolve to do one thing this summer. I would tell Tina about Miriam. It hadn't seemed important before, but it felt like the right thing now. The hurt and anger were long gone. The memory was softer, and I often hoped Miriam was happy with the life she had chosen.

The town was slowly but steadily growing to the west and south. The older section to the east remained the same. I arrived about five in the morning just as the diner was opening. Helen was there and gave me a hug and a menu. I was hungry and ate a farmer's breakfast of ham, eggs, hash-browns, toast and coffee. I bought a local paper and checked the ads for apartments for rent.

Helen noticed and said, "It looks like you plan to stick around a while this time. That will make a lot of people here happy, one in particular."

I told her about the last letter from Tina. She was studying hard for her finals and would graduate the first Saturday in June. Yes, I would be there, and no, I would not wear a necktie or a suit.

Pete was glad to see me and was interested in my goal of learning to be a mason.

"First, you will have to serve an apprenticeship under a certified mason," he said. "And that could take two to three years. There are three main types of masons—block masons, brick masons and stone masons. On top of that, you have to learn to read a blueprint."

I knew he wasn't trying to talk me out of it, he just wanted me to understand the long progression of training I would have to go through.

After letting me think about it for a minute, he said, "I can set you up with Henry who is my top mason. We can split your time working for me and with him. All I need is your word that after you get certified you give me one year's work in trade."

We shook hands, and the deal was sealed.

I started that Monday by calling the local VFW and finding Pete two new guys to replace one guy who quit and one in jail for D&D. Then I took the delivery truck to the garage and had it tuned up and the oil changed. I had things pretty well organized by noon and went out on-site to meet Henry.

He was about 50 and in better shape than I was. As he shook my hand, he said, "Pete tells me you are a quick study. Let's find out how quick."

He took me through the basics and explained he only did brick and block, no stone. I learned there were different types of brick and block and each had its own pattern. He did a quick layout for me, and I wondered if I could master this.

Discerning what I was thinking, Henry said, "Always start your corners first. This will help keep your line straight, and you can eyeball your progress as you go."

For the first few days, I carried a lot of block and learned more about mud than I thought I knew. I watched and learned. On the third day, I laid my first block. I was hooked. This was what I wanted to do, and I was determined to learn.

* * *

The first Saturday in June was a hot, sunny day filled with the sounds and sights of nervous students and parents. Blue caps and gowns flashed through the crowd as everyone made their way to the auditorium. I took a seat with Sally, her boyfriend Andrew and Tina's parents, Cora and David.

They were happy to see me and asked if I were going to stay this time.

"I have decided to make your town my town," I said.

Patting me on the shoulder, Cora said, "Everyone wants you to stay, specially Tina."

David, who was the assistant manager of the local John Deere dealership, nodded his head in agreement.

The music started, the spotlights went on the stage and the graduates filed in. All the faces were a blur except one. Tina looked radiant. Her dark red hair framed her lovely face, and she held her head high with a satisfied look. We were as proud of her as she was of herself.

Once the speeches and ceremonies were over, the crowd burst into a cheer. The graduates joined their families, and it seemed everyone was hugging everyone.

After turning in her gown, we met Tina outside, and she was bursting with her news.

"I got a job as a feature reporter for the Lincoln newspaper," she gushed out. "I start Monday at $200 a week plus expenses, but I have to be here during the week."

I smiled and looked over at her dad. "I think between David and I we can locate a good used-car for you so you don't have to walk home every weekend," I said. As a matter of fact, we already had a car for her parked at home. It was her graduation present.

After a quick lunch, Sally, Andrew and Tina's parents headed back home. Tina and I loaded all her things into my truck and were about to take off when she said coyly, "We don't have to drive straight home do we?"

The nearest motel was out on the highway. We stopped at the first one and checked in. The afternoon was spent catching up on some together time. In between the bouts of love-making, we talked about the coming summer and how we planned to spend the time.

As we lay there, enjoying the closeness of each other, I felt it was time to tell her about Miriam. I got the story out in one long confession. Tina never interrupted, just listened.

When I was finished, she said, "That is so sad. I feel like I want to do something to make it better, but I'm also glad she found God and I found you. I think this is the way it is supposed to be. Do you still have feelings for her?"

I kissed her softly and said, "The only feelings I have for her are for her happiness. I think you are absolutely right about us finding each other. Maybe someday I will be able to put it right, but it won't be anytime soon."

The rest of the afternoon passed in a cloud of dark red hair, green eyes and soft lips.

Tina loved the car. It was a five-year-old Chevy with low mileage and new tires.

I had found a small apartment on the east side of town and was trying to find some furniture to put in it. So far, I had a bed and a dresser but not much else. Tina and I spent weekends going to garage sales and soon had a couch, an end table, a coffee table, a recliner, a small TV and some lamps. She bought some pictures for the walls and some old cookware of her mother's. It was like she was moving in without moving in. Every time she showed up with some new article the little voice in my head would yell, 'Go, Tina!'

One Friday afternoon, when I got home from work, she was hanging up some of her clothes in my closet. My little voice almost blew out one of my eardrums. 'Go Tina!'

One day I asked her, "How do your parents feel about you spending so much time over here?"

She took hold of the front of my shirt, and looking me straight in the eyes, said, "My parents and I agree that you are the best thing in my life. When I'm happy, they are happy."

On the occasional weekend that Tina had to work in Lincoln, we would spend time there in her apartment shared with another girl. We explored the small corners of Lincoln to avoid crowds and maybe find a human interest story for Tina.

We woke up early one Sunday morning. The sun was melting away the last of the overnight shadows, and birds were chirping.

I said to Tina, "We never talked about what religion you were born into."

With a lazy smile, she said, "I guess I was born Lutheran, but my folks never attended on a regular basis. I used to go once in a while, but when I got to college, I was just too busy. Why do you ask?"

"I was just thinking if you don't mind, let's go to church," I said.

With a smile, she said, "Which church—yours or mine?"

"Let's go to yours," I said. "I want to see if Lutherans worship like Catholics."

While she showered, I made some coffee, then took my turn getting ready. Once, when I was six years old, I asked my dad why we always went to the same place for church.

"The other church in town is Lutheran, and if a Catholic sets foot in a Lutheran church God will strike them with a bolt of lightning," he said with a very serious look.

Today I would find out if God really cared where people worshiped.

As it turned out, he didn't send down a bolt of lightning. We prayed, we sang and we held hands while we listened to the sermon. It was peaceful and pleasant.

As we left, Tina said, "I enjoyed that, let's do it more often."

Later, we had brunch at her parents' house, and Tina told them we had been to church. Cora smiled, and David nodded his head. He seemed to do that a lot when he was in a good mood. I guess David did his talking at work and Cora did the talking at home.

Chapter Twelve

ANOTHER FOURTH OF JULY had rolled around, but for Tina and me, this one would be different. We were going to see my parents. She had been asking for weeks if we could go, but I was a little hesitant.

Finally, Tina said, "If we are ever going to be really up front with each other I have to meet your family. The fourth falls on a Sunday. Pete will give you Monday off, and we are leaving Friday afternoon." She gave me that 'or else' look, and I knew playtime was over.

We packed light and left town about five o'clock. It was 500 miles to my hometown. Traffic was heavy until about eight o'clock then thinned out somewhere in Iowa. We stopped for gas, and a quick burger then hit the road again.

Just after midnight, we crossed the Wisconsin state line and took a break at a truck stop. After a light breakfast, we napped in the truck for about an hour and drove on.

At seven o'clock Saturday morning, I drove into my parents' driveway and parked. Dad was just getting ready to go to work at the warehouse where he was the forklift driver.

"About time you showed up," he said. "I'll be home at four, and I'm taking the family out for supper."

I introduced him to Tina and asked about my brother.

"Your mom will tell you all about that lazy drunk," he said and left for work.

Mom had been expecting us and had hot coffee and cinnamon rolls waiting. It had been about a year and a half since I had seen her last, but she looked about five years older. There were lines and wrinkles around her eyes, and she had lost some weight. She gushed over Tina and asked all about her family.

As I watched them, I got the feeling there was something bothering Mom. I remembered what my dad had said about the 'lazy drunk' and decided to raise the subject.

"How are Tim and Connie doing?" I asked.

Mom got that worried look on her face and said, "Connie is seven months pregnant, and Tim lost his job at the pallet factory. If they can't meet the rent payment this week, they lose their apartment."

"Dad said Tim has been drinking pretty heavy; is that true?" I asked.

"Yes he has, that's how he lost his job," she said.

As Mom and I talked, Tina had been silent. Now she said, "Are Connie and the baby doing all right?"

"Oh yes, they are just fine," Mom said, "but Connie has just about had enough of Tim. I'm afraid they may be splitting up if Tim doesn't straighten up soon."

I was getting the feeling this was not going to be the happy family reunion Tina and I had hoped for.

I knew my parents would not be happy about Tina and me sleeping together under their Catholic roof, so I told mom we were going to stay at a motel. We left and checked into the nearest motel and without even undressing, laid down and slept for two hours.

When I awoke, Tina was still sleeping. I lay there quietly and let my mind drift back to when I had left here over a year ago. My folks were the same but older. My brother was the same but dumber. The town was the same but not my home anymore.

Tina snored softly, her breath gently stirring the three hairs on my chest. I knew Tim liked to drink, but from what Mom said it was getting out of hand. A father-to-be needed to be more responsible. I would talk to him and see what the problem was. When I looked down, Tina was staring up at me.

"Are you going to talk to your brother?" she asked.

"Stop reading my mind; it's spooky," I answered.

We got up and stretched to work the kinks out.

"If we are going out to eat, we should shower and change T-shirts," she said.

"Sorry, we can't," I answered.

"Why not?" she said with a puzzled look.

"Because your T-shirt won't fit me," I answered with a chuckle.

She laughed, threw her T-shirt at me and walked into the small bathroom.

We got back to the house at five o'clock. Dad was home, all showered and shaved and sitting at the picnic table in the small back yard. Tina stayed in the house talking to Mom, I got a beer out of the fridge and joined Dad.

"What's with Tim and the drinking?' I asked.

Dad gave me a sideways look and said, "He is still a twenty-seven-year-old kid. He could hardly deal with marriage, and now he's got a baby on the way. Lately, he and Connie have been fighting like cats and dogs. She yells at him for being a bum, and he yells at her for being a ball-busting bitch. Trouble is, they're both right."

We laughed together at that, and it felt good to share something with Dad, even if it was bad news.

Mom and Tina walked out, and Mom said, "Connie called. They will meet us at the steak-house at six."

Mom didn't drink, but Tina had found a beer in the fridge, took a long pull at it and let out a very unladylike belch. Dad laughed and asked, "Do all the girls in Nebraska drink like that?"

Tina winked at him and answered, "They do if they date your son."

With a wide grin, Dad looked at me and said, "You got a keeper here, boy; if you let her go you're an idiot."

We met Tim and Connie in the parking lot of the steak-house. Connie looked pretty but very pregnant. Tim looked like he got an early start on the celebration. I hugged Connie and shook hands with Tim. He couldn't take his eyes off of Tina.

"Are there any more in Nebraska like you?" he asked her.

"You bet there are," Tina said with a grin, "and if you stay here, they will stay there."

Tim blushed red, and Connie and Dad shared a good laugh. Dad had picked this place because they didn't serve beer, and Tim wanted to go somewhere else.

"If you're buying, we will go anywhere you can afford," Dad said.

Tim backed down, and we went in to eat. It was typical steak-house food, but it was also special because we were together. Tina kept us entertained with stories of college life and some of the stories she had covered as a reporter.

As we left, Tina was behind me, and Tim was behind her. Going out the door, I heard her give a little yelp of surprise. When we got to the car, Tina turned around and said, "I have something for you, Tim."

He walked over to her with a smirk on his face. As he got closer, Tina drove a knee into his crotch. His eyes got big as he let out a grunt and dropped to the ground. Mom and Connie gasped, and Dad had that what-the-hell-happened look on his face.

Tina looked at us and said, "He pinched my ass on the way out the door. I'm betting he won't do that again."

Dad and I were laughing as we loaded Tim in his car and a very red-faced Connie got behind the wheel and drove off. We said goodnight to my parents and went back to the motel.

On Sunday morning, we slept until nine and had breakfast at a downtown diner. My parents would be at church until noon, and later we would go watch the parade of veterans down Main Street.

As we finished eating, I said, "Let's take a drive over to Tim and Connie's. I want to see if he has recovered from his etiquette lesson."

Tina said, "Sure, let's go."

As we drove up to their apartment, we saw Connie loading clothes into their car. Tim was sitting in a chair outside watching her and drinking a beer.

"Looks like we caught you on moving day," I said.

"I'm leaving that lazy bum and moving back to my parents' house," Connie said. She turned and went back into the apartment and Tina followed to help.

"That crazy bitch doesn't know when she has it good," Tim said with a belch.

"Seems more like she knows when she has it bad," I replied.

"Shut up and mind your own business," Tim said. Aand by the way, you ought to teach the wildcat of yours some manners."

"Oh, she has manners," I replied, "that's why your sore balls are still between your legs. Tina wanted to hang them on my rear-view mirror."

Tim's hand shook a little bit as he said, "She wouldn't dare."

"She not only would dare, I would hold you down while she cut them off," I said.

His glazed eyes stared at me as he snarled "Get out of my life and stay out."

Tina and Connie were loading the last of her stuff in the car. I walked over and gave Connie a hug.

"If he gives you any trouble, call my dad," I said.

We waited until Connie drove away then got in my truck and left.

The parade was great. I recognized a few of the older guys and none of the younger ones. There were some floats from local businesses, a few clowns throwing candy, the local beauty queen and two politicians running for office. The whole thing wound up at the fairgrounds where a carnival was in progress.

Mom and Tina explored the hand-crafted knick-knacks in the long line of booths set up on the grass. Dad and I talked. He was interested in my becoming a mason. He asked questions that I actually had answers for. We joked back and forth and had a soft drink in the shade of an oak tree, waiting for our women.

"Have you told Tina you're in love with her?' he asked.

"No, we haven't gotten that far in our relationship yet," I answered.

"That's bullshit," Dad said, "you're just afraid to take the step because you think you might get your little heart broke again. I can tell when I see you together that she loves you, so be a man and tell her."

When did my dad get so smart, I wondered. To change the subject I asked, "Have you or Mom heard anything about Miriam?"

"She is in a novitiate somewhere in Indiana," Dad said. "From what her mother told us, she will become a nun next March."

Mom and Tina walked up arm in arm carrying bags of trinkets and giggling over something. We all walked back to Dad's car and drove home.

We left the motel about six o'clock. We decided to take our time driving back. We motored along until nine, then pulled into a motel and checked in. We dumped our bags in the room and walked to the restaurant next to the motel. After we ordered we talked.

"Your mom would like to visit Nebraska someday," Tina told me.

"I don't think she has ever been across the state line," I said.

"I like your parents," she said. "Your mom is cute in her own way, and you're dad is a hoot. What he is thinking just comes right out of his mouth. Has he always been like that?"

I laughed and said, "Once, when I was eight years old, Dad waited on the church steps after Mass. After everybody left, he told the priest that although he had a nice baritone voice, his sermons were boring. Dad told him to throw in a clean joke once in a while to liven things up. After that people used to go to church just to hear the sermons."

As we lay in bed that night, I got to thinking about what my dad had said. Maybe it was time to tell Tina how I felt about her.

I was just about to open my mouth when Tina sat up and said, "I have to tell you something. We have never mentioned the word, but I think it's time I tell you that I am in love with you. No matter how you feel, that one fact will not change."

For a half-minute, I just stared at her, then said, "I was about to tell you that I was in love with *you*, but you beat me to it. It's like our minds are on the same wavelength. I have known I loved you since the Christmas I came back from Texas. I didn't tell you because I didn't want to scare you away."

"That's when I knew too!" she yelled. "I didn't tell you then because I was afraid you wouldn't come back from Texas!"

"Well, now that we know, what do we do about it?" I asked.

With a coy wink, Tina said, "How about we spend the night proving our love?"

Chapter Thirteen

WE FINISHED WORK on the subdivision at the end of July. The only things left were the carpet company and the landscaper.

Henry had me laying block on my own now, occasionally making a comment on keeping the mortar moist or holding my trowel a certain way. Overall, he seemed pleased with my work and let Pete know.

My paycheck had increased, and I was steadily banking the money. I had a long-range plan that would need some capital. Tina had totally moved in to my apartment now, and the closet could hardly hold both our clothes. Her sister Sally and her fiancé Andrew had finally set a wedding date for May of next year.

My boss Pete had two crews working now and had contracted for an apartment complex on the west side of town. I took a drive with him one Saturday morning to look at the site. What had once been a cornfield would now become residential housing.

"I want to give it a different look," Pete said thoughtfully.

"Why not go with an Old West style?" I said.

Pete's face lit up with a grin. "That's a great idea," he said. "I could even put in hitching rails and give the office a 'general store' look."

We walked the property while Pete took notes on his clipboard. On the way home, Pete asked if Tina and I wanted to come over for supper.

With a grin, I told him, "Can't this weekend, Pete—Tina is staying in Lincoln. It seems the mayor and his secretary dipped into the city treasury and took off for parts unknown. The newspaper is trying to track them down. Tina thinks they went to Las Vegas and she is hot on their trail."

With a laugh, Pete said, "If anyone can find them it will be Tina."

My Ford truck had been making some noises I didn't like so I decided to trade it in. Saturday afternoon, I picked out a white extended cab Chevy Silverado with low mileage and new tires. As I signed the papers, I thought this was the perfect opportunity to test drive it all the way to Lincoln and surprise Tina. I filled it with gas and took off.

Two hours later, I was sitting in front of the newspaper office. The truck ran smooth as silk and rode like a dream. When I walked in, I saw Tina sitting at a desk, talking on the phone and waving her arm in the air to make some point. She saw me and broke into a big smile and hung up.

She ran over to me and whispered, "How much do you love me?"

I extended my arms all the way out and said, "This much is just the beginning."

"Would that include a long drive to Denver?" she asked quietly.

"California would be about halfway," I answered.

She grabbed my arm and dragged me to a quiet spot in a corner. Still whispering, she said, "The mayor and his hussy did go to Las Vegas. They lost about half the money they stole playing blackjack. The hussy got scared and demanded the mayor drive her home."

She stopped to take a breath and continued. "They stopped in Denver overnight at a ritzy hotel, and the mayor got drunk in the bar and picked a fight with the bartender who was hitting on the hussy. My friend Marcy from journalism school works for the Denver paper. She heard about the fight and the arrest on her police scanner. That's who I was talking to when you walked in."

Tina put both hands on my chest and gave me that pleading look that I never could resist. "The paper will pay for the gas if you drive me to Denver. We can scoop the other papers if I can interview the mayor in jail in Denver."

I leaned over and whispered in her ear, "Go to the restroom before we leave."

She gave a little squeal, grabbed her purse and jacket and ran to the ladies room.

It's about a 500-mile trip from Lincoln to Denver. Tina slept while I drove. We made it in thirteen hours. We parked in The Denver Police Department lot at six in the morning.

Tina flashed her press credentials, and the jailer led her back to the cell while I sat out front and drank some really bad coffee. An hour later, Tina came out, motioned to me, and we stepped outside.

"The secretary is still at the hotel wondering how to get home. I can interview her, then we can take her to the bus station here. The police will meet her in Lincoln if I call them from here."

The plump blonde woman who answered the hotel door looked like she had been crying all night. I left Tina with her and went to the breakfast bar. By ten o'clock that morning we had the hussy on a bus non-stop for Lincoln.

I pulled out on the highway not long after the bus left. Stopping for gas and coffee twice we drove straight through to Lincoln, arriving just after midnight. I dropped Tina at the paper and drove to her apartment. I was dead tired and fell onto her bed. I set her alarm for three a.m. and slept like a dead man. When the alarm went off, I got up, showered and got dressed. Her roommate had coffee waiting. I took one to go and hit the road and got to the worksite with five minutes to spare.

Tina's story beat every other newspaper and also the local TV and radio stations. The mayor had been brought back to Lincoln by the police, and his lawyer stopped him from talking anymore to the press. The television showed a short fat guy with an almost bald head being led from a car to the jail. The secretary was already there and telling the reporters how this awful man had deceived her and led her astray. Tina got a raise. I got a sore ass from driving a thousand miles for love, and for Tina, I would do it again.

For the next two weeks, I talked to Tina on the phone about every other day. Then the story died down, and one Friday afternoon when I got home from work, Tina was there. The table was set with candles and wine. She met me at the door with a long kiss that I had been missing.

"You have no idea how much I missed you," she said. "But for the next two days, I am going to reward you with whatever your heart desires."

"My heart desires your undivided attention for two days," I answered.

"I have something for you from the newspaper," she said. She picked up an envelope from the table and handed it to me. I opened it and inside was a letter from her editor and a check for $500. The letter explained it was for mileage and expenses.

"You work for a very nice newspaper," I said. Then I smelled a wonderful odor wafting from the small oven.

"I'm making you my famous lasagna, and then we will catch up on current events," Tina said with that sexy wink she only used when she had some special events planned.

* * *

The new subdivision with the Old West design was in demand before it was half-built. The local weekly newspaper did a full page spread on the construction and interviewed Pete to get the story behind it and when it would be completed. Before it was half-finished, all the units were spoken for.

I worked a lot on my own now. Henry showed up each day to inspect the work and make notes in his journal. Masonry was not only an art form to me, it allowed me to actually see structure being formed from raw material.

By the first of September, the weather began to change for the worse. Days of heavy wind and driving rain put us behind schedule. During these times Henry and I would meet at the trailer office. From a stack of cardboard tubes, Henry selected a few and began teaching me to read blueprints. He suggested I take a course on reading blueprints at the college in Lincoln over the winter. It was sound advice that I intended to follow through on.

The trial for the wayward mayor and his babe-in-arms started the second week in October. Tina would be covering it every day and giving me updates over the phone. The mayor swore that his secretary, Linda, was the brains of the whole thing. It was her idea to steal the money and go to Las Vegas. He didn't want to play blackjack, but she made him do it.

According to Linda, the hussy, the mayor planned the whole thing just to get in her lace undies. He planned to triple their money at the blackjack table and flee to Mexico. The jury decided they were equally guilty. They both got seven years and were ordered to sell their assets to pay back the money. The mayor's wife had divorced him and won the house and car in the settlement, so he had no assets. The secretary said she only had one asset and state law forbids her to sell it. She did offer it to her attorney in exchange for his fee, but he declined the offer. The press was having a field day with the whole affair, and the town was outraged at the lack of morals of their public officials. The town treasurer was named acting mayor until election time next year.

CHAPTER FOURTEEN

W E HAD NOTICED THE DOG hanging around the last few days. He looked like a Jack Russell, but it was hard to tell without getting a closer look. One morning as I left for work, I grabbed two plastic bowls and a can of beef stew from the cupboard and put them in the truck. When I got to the worksite, I filled one bowl with water and one with the beef stew. I set them down at the edge of the parking area and went to work.

About ten o'clock, I looked up, and the dog was eating like it was his first meal in days. He licked the bowl clean, drank some water and laid down to watch us work. When we broke for lunch, he was still there watching.

"If you keep feeding him, he will follow you home," Pete said with a smile.

Henry walked over and tossed the dog a half of a sandwich which got a good sniff and then disappeared down its throat.

One of the carpenters noticed it didn't have a collar. "Maybe somebody dumped it off," he said.

I liked the look of this little mutt. "If I owned a dog that looked like that I would name it Jack," I told Pete.

"Call him and see what happens," Pete said.

I gave a little whistle and called, "Come here, Jack." To my surprise, the dog walked over and sniffed my hand. I scratched him behind the ears which made him close his eyes and roll his head. I got up and refilled the water bowl and went back to work. Jack picked a spot in the shade and laid down for a nap.

At four o'clock, I cleaned my trowel, washed the mortar board and called it a day. I picked up the plastic dishes and put them in the truck. Jack was sitting in the shade watching all this. I guess right then I made up my mind to see if he needed a home.

Holding the truck door open, I called out, "Let's go, Jack."

Without hesitation, the dog trotted over, leaped into the truck and sat in the passenger seat like he knew he was going home.

The first stop was the pet store for a collar, leash, shampoo, a bag of dog food, water and food bowls and a box of biscuits. Next was the vet to set up an appointment for shots and a checkup. During all this, Jack patiently waited in the truck with the windows open.

When we got to my apartment, I called him out of the truck. He inspected the small yard and picked a likely spot to call his and baptized it. I unlocked the door and held it open for him. He entered slowly and sniffed all the furniture. He checked the bathroom, kitchen and bedroom, wagging his tail the whole time.

As I filled his bowls with water and food, he sat patiently until I set them on the floor in the corner. After he ate, he paid a visit to his spot outdoors and then trotted back in the apartment. Apparently, he had decided to stick around.

Next came the bath. He must have been through this routine before because he sat in the tub and enjoyed the whole thing. After drying him off, I took an old blanket from the closet and laid it in the corner of the bedroom. He sniffed it, pawed it into a proper sleeping shape and laid down.

"Welcome home, Jack," I said and turned out the light.

The apartment manager was a nice lady named Adele who informed me that dogs were not allowed. Since I rented the place by the month, with no lease, I told her I would take care of it when I got home. I gave a short whistle, Jack jumped in the truck, and we left for work.

It was Friday, and the day was warm with a light breeze that made the hours pass quickly. At four, Jack and I set off to find a new place to live. The local paper advertised several houses on the east side of town, so we headed in that direction.

What caught my eye was a post-war ranch-style, two bedroom with a garage and a back yard. I wrote down the address and phone number of the real estate company, and we drove back into town.

The office was right on Main Street, and as I drove up, a middle-aged man was just locking up.

"I want to rent the house on Drake street," I yelled out.

The man stopped, smiled and said, "I was just about to head home, but let's take care of this for you."

The house rented by the month and was only twenty dollars more per month than the apartment. He said there would be no problem with having a dog. I signed the papers and gave him the first month's rent plus a deposit. He handed me the keys, shook my hand, and we both left. He went home, and Jack and I went to give Adele the good news.

As we drove up to the apartment, I saw Tina's car parked there.

"Now you get to meet the lady of the house," I told Jack.

As I was getting out of the truck, Tina opened the apartment door and stepped out. Jack's ears went up, but his tail was wagging.

"Come over here, Tina, I've got a surprise for you," I called.

As she got closer, she saw Jack. "Where did you get that cute dog?" she squealed. She knelt down, and Jack went right to her. His tail was wagging so fast I was afraid his rear end would lift off the ground. Tina was talking baby talk to him, and he was loving it.

Looking up at me, Tina asked, "Does Adele know about him?"

"She told me this morning that no dogs were allowed," I answered.

"What are we going to do?" Tina moaned.

"It's pretty simple really" I answered. "We are moving this weekend to a house I just rented. Want to go take a look at it?"

Tina ran around to the passenger side with Jack right behind her. She opened the door, got in, and Jack jumped up and landed in her lap.

"I think my dog just became *our* dog," I said, and we drove to the new house.

"It's perfect for us," Tina said as we walked through the front door. The living room was newly carpeted, and the kitchen was tile-floored. The rest of the rooms and the hallway were hardwood floors. The basement was unfinished, but there was a washer and dryer and a work bench with a light over it.

"We can wait until tomorrow, or we can spend the night moving in," I said.

"Let's go start packing," Tina said. "Jack needs a place to sleep tonight."

We drove back to the apartment, and I knocked on Adele's door. She opened it, stepped out and said "I can't change the rules for one tenant. You will have to get rid of the dog."

With a smile, I answered, "Jack is leaving, and so am I. We will be moving out tonight. You can send my security deposit to our new address."

Her jaw dropped, and her eyes got big. This was not the answer she had been expecting.

"I'll leave the keys on the kitchen counter," I told her and went to pack up. I don't know where Tina got the energy to move in non-stop motion all night.

"You start with the furniture, and I will start in the kitchen and bathroom," she yelled over her shoulder as I walked in the door. It took four truckloads and six hours, but by midnight we were moved in. The new house looked like a yard sale gone wild. We slept on the mattress on the floor with Jack stretched out at the foot end of the mattress.

By Saturday afternoon, everything was set up and in place. Jack followed Tina around like he was on an invisible leash. All the while, she spoke to him like she was expecting an answer. She did get an occasional 'woof' which made her giggle like a little girl.

Tina looked around at the sparse living room and shook her head. "Let's go raid my parents' garage," she said. "They have my bedroom furniture there that we need for the other bedroom."

"Woof," I answered.

She furrowed her brow and gave me that are-you-nuts look.

"I guess it only works with Jack," I said with a smile.

Realizing what I was doing, she started laughing. She tackled me, and we ended up on the floor with Jack on top of us.

Tina's mom went goofy over Jack. As we loaded the bed, dresser and small desk in the truck, Cora was feeding him bits of leftover roast beef from the night before.

"Does my little doggy want some more treat?" she cooed at him.

Jack was doing things I didn't know he could do. Sitting up, walking in circles on his hind legs and rolling over on his back only encouraged Cora to make more of a fuss over him.

"If I moved out today she probably wouldn't even notice until bedtime," David said with a laugh.

We stayed for supper and caught up on what was happening in town. David told us that since the town treasury was depleted, the town board was trying to push through an emergency tax to build it back up.

"The problem is the townspeople don't want to pay for the mayor's affair," said David.

"I think the town is going to get its money back," Tina said with a grin. "It seems the mayor owns a sizeable chunk of real estate registered under his wife's maiden name. The town can take it over as an asset, sell it and pay back almost all the money he stole."

We left around six o'clock. Jack was so full of roast beef I had to lift him into the truck.

"You come back and visit me soon, sweetie," Cora said with a kiss.

"Are you talking to me or the dog?" Tina asked with a grin.

"Well, of course, I meant you, honey, but be sure to bring my little sweetums with you," Cora said, blushing a bright pink.

We set up the bed in the second bedroom and bought in the dresser and desk.

"Now we need to get you some new bedding, towels, curtains and a few more lamps," Tina said.

"Finding a home for a dog is a lot more expensive than I thought it would be," I replied, scratching my head.

I looked around for Jack and finally found him sleeping off his roast beef binge. He was spread out on his blanket in the bedroom, snoring.

Tina left at five o'clock Monday morning for the drive back to Lincoln. The sky was overcast like a storm might be brewing. The wind was picking up as Jack and I left for work.

By eight o'clock, the rain started, and the sky was a dark gray with black clouds rolling overhead. The air felt thick and heavy with moisture. Then the rain stopped, and the air got quiet. The apartment unit we were working on had the shell up and the roof on. Pete came around and very quietly ordered everyone into the basement of the unit. I whistled for Jack, and he came running.

"I heard on the radio in the office there were tornadoes spotted to the west," he said, "and we are going to stay here until the weather clears."

Then we heard the most terrible sound we'd ever experienced. There was a grinding, ripping, tearing sound mixed with a thunderous roar. It lasted for about five minutes but seemed like hours. Then, suddenly, it was quiet.

One of the men started for the steps, and Pete yelled "Stop right there! This isn't over yet. We could be in the eye of the storm, with more to come."

Thankfully, it was over. We knew when we heard the birds calling. Slowly, Pete made his way up the steps and lifted off the plywood we had laid over the hole. The sun was shining, and the air felt clean. The unit we were in was still standing, but not much else was.

We looked around for our vehicles, but there were none in sight. What few small trees had been there were gone. To our right had been two almost completed units. Now they were a tangled mess of broken and splintered wood and asphalt shingles.

"You men head for home the best way you can," Pete said, "but remember that tornado is still in front of you, so be careful."

Because of the broken glass littering the gravel drive I carried Jack out to the blacktop highway. Across the highway in a field, laying on its side, was my Chevy truck. All the glass was gone, the hood was gone, the frame was bent at an impossible angle, and one front wheel was missing. I salvaged what I could and continued down the highway. The twister had wandered across the landscape leaving a path of destruction a half-mile wide.

I heard the wail of a siren and saw a police car bearing down on me. I stopped and waved it down. I told him where we had been working and that everyone was okay.

"We are spread out all over, and if you could ride with me in case I need assistance, I sure would appreciate it," he said.

"If you don't mind some canine company I'll be glad to," I replied.

We drove as close to the path of the twister as we could and stopped to help as needed. There were trees down on houses, power lines down everywhere and people wandering around looking dazed and confused. A mother was carrying a young boy with a broken arm. We took both in the back of the car and drove to the hospital and dropped them off.

A call came over the police car radio about people trapped in a blown-down house. We took off again and found the house with people standing around.

"Is anyone inside?" asked the officer.

A firefighter standing nearby said, "We can't account for a woman and her baby, but we get no answer when we call out to her."

Jack jumped out of the cruiser and ran to the side of the debris and started barking and digging. As if on cue, four of us ran over and began throwing broken lumber aside. A part of what was left standing looked like it may have been a closet. As we got the wreckage cleared away, we saw a woman laying on her side covering a baby with her body. There was a bloody gash on her head, but she was breathing. The baby seemed awfully quiet, but when I touched it, the eyes opened, and it started wailing. As we carried them out, someone snapped a picture with a camera. The officer and I loaded the mother in the back of the car, and I held the baby as we drove back to the hospital. Jack sat in the back gently licking the woman's arm. We heard later they would both be fine.

It was near midnight before we took a break at the police station. The officers were treating Jack like a hero for finding the mother and baby. A reporter took a picture of me, Jack and the officer.

I found a phone not being used and called the newspaper office in Lincoln and asked for Tina.

"Are you all right?" she asked like she was holding back the tears.

"Jack and I are fine," I answered, "but my truck is wrecked."

"How bad is the damage to the town?" Tina asked.

"It took a half-mile swath out of the southwest part of town, skipped over the town itself and took a corner of the eastside, then went back up and disappeared into thin air," I said.

"Are my parents all right, and is our house still there?" she asked.

"I called David, and he and Cora are fine. The tornado lifted up before it got to them. It missed our house too. When can you get back here?" I asked.

"I may be here over the weekend to cover all the stories coming in. I'll call and let you know," said Tina.

It would be a week and a half before I saw her again.

Jack was a local hero. The papers all loved dog stories, and Jack was a natural ham for the camera. He was made an honorary police officer and an honorary firefighter.

At night, he would wander around the house looking for Tina. When she finally did get home, he was so happy he tinkled on the kitchen floor. Tina thought it was so cute! Knowing I would not get the same reaction, I restrained my bladder.

Tina said according to all the reports it would take six months just to clean everything up after the twister. The total cost was still being tabulated. No one had died, but several were injured, two seriously.

Pete and every other local contractor put their projects on hold and went to work rebuilding the town. The insurance company came through for me, and I got another Chevy truck. It was a year newer extended cab painted baby blue.

Tina, Jack and I were in the driveway washing it down one Saturday afternoon when a two-door sedan pulled in behind the truck. A young man and a woman carrying a baby got out and walked over. I had never seen him before, but she looked vaguely familiar. He stuck out his hand and said, "My name is Brian, and this is my wife Mary and our son Billy. We want to thank you and your dog for saving her life."

Then I recognized her! She was the woman Jack had found in the blown-down house!

"You're more than welcome, sir, but it was Jack who found them," I said.

The woman bent down, and Jack gave her a lick on the cheek and gave the baby one on the arm.

Tina, of course, had to 'ooh' and 'ah' over the baby. Brian told me he was a long-haul trucker and had been on the road in Utah when the tornado hit.

We invited them to stay for supper, but they were on their way to Mary's folks' place for the weekend. As they drove away, I told Tina, "It's nice to have at least one happy ending to that terrible day."

CHAPTER FIFTEEN

THANKSGIVING DAY WAS SPENT with Tina's parents. While Tina and her mom were busy in the kitchen, Jack, David and I watched the Detroit Lions and the Kansas City Chiefs battle on the field.

My mind drifted back to other Thanksgivings with my family. Before Dad sold the farm for back taxes, the family was lucky to have a chicken and some potatoes. After we moved to town, things got better. Through it all, Mom never complained, but she sure prayed a lot. Dad was a hard worker, and as he got promoted, things got better.

"Mom, you have to stop feeding Jack at the table," Tina said in a pleading tone.

"But my little sweetums is hungry," Cora said sadly.

I looked at Jack with a frown. "Go lay down, you little beggar," I said sternly.

With his tail in the air, he walked over, jumped on the couch and closed his eyes.

Cora had made enough food for a dozen people. A twenty-pound turkey, dressing, mashed potatoes, gravy, green bean casserole, sweet potatoes, two kinds of cranberries, three kinds of pie, and butter and egg rolls.

"This Christmas, Tina and I would like to host a dinner all of us," I said with a smile.

It had been Tina's idea, and I was all for it.

"That's a wonderful idea," Cora said. "Don't you think so, David?"

"I will look forward to it," David said with a smile.

By the time Detroit had squeaked out a win over the Chiefs, Cora and Tina had divided the leftovers. It took two trips to carry it all out to the truck. Jack waddled out behind us, and I had to lift him into the truck, again.

* * *

Pete planned to work right through the winter this year for two reasons—we needed to get the people whose houses had been destroyed into their new homes as soon as possible, and we had to catch up on the contract work to meet the deadline. This winter I would be swinging a hammer and climbing ladders.

Tina was still working out of Lincoln for *The Journal Star*. She had started taking Jack to work once a week, and he had become the office mascot. Her editor was a dog lover who sometimes bought his cocker spaniel to work with him. Jack and the spaniel got along great, and Tina was encouraged to bring Jack more often. Jack had no objections.

The second weekend in December, the three of us went shopping for our Christmas tree. It was about six foot tall and had a beautiful shape. The guy at the tree lot remembered the stories of Jack in the paper and threw in a free Christmas wreath.

We had to buy ornaments, lights, garland and an angel for the top of the tree.

"I don't know what to buy Jack for a present," Tina wailed.

"How about a treadmill so he can work off the excess pounds from all those treats he's been getting at work?" I chimed in.

I got a punch in the arm for my idea.

We got the tree home, and I sawed off a few branches at the bottom to make room for the presents later. We spent the afternoon and part of the evening decorating our first Christmas tree together. A few Tom & Jerry's later, we plugged in the light and marveled at the beauty of our creation.

We went to church Christmas eve. Friends shook hands and hugged each other. Cards were exchanged, and small gifts were stuffed into coat pockets. The message of the Mass was the same as it had been for hundreds of years— peace on Earth beginning with the birth of a child.

As we filed out, there was a light snow falling. By morning it would add up to six inches of white wonder.

Christmas morning began with letting Jack out and making coffee. I was nervous. I had made a major decision, and I hoped it would be received kindly.

Jack got a rawhide bone which he proceeded to devour. Tina handed me a package that felt like clothing. It was a University of Nebraska sweatshirt with a hood.

"That will fit under your work jacket and keep you warm at work," she said with a big smile.

I handed her a small square box with a bow on it. She opened it and gasped. It was an engagement ring.

"The date is not important, but the answer is," I said. "Will you marry me?"

She actually shrieked, "YES!"

She tackled me to the floor with tears dripping from her long lashes. "I love you so much my heart can't hold it all," she sniffled.

"Me too," I added.

She jumped up and ran into the kitchen yelling "I have to call my mom, then Sally!"

I sat drinking coffee and watched Jack gnaw on his bone.

Cora and David arrived about ten o'clock to help with the dinner. Sally made a visit to see the ring and give us both a hug. The women hugged and cried while David and I sat in the living room talking and drinking coffee.

Later, the smell of the hickory-smoked ham cooking in the oven wafted through the house. Along with the ham, we had scalloped potatoes, fruit salad, cornbread and bread pudding for dessert.

Jack lay by Cora's chair where an occasional piece of ham made it's way to the floor. Everyone was on their way home by two o'clock. I helped put away food and dry the dishes.

A very tired but happy Tina stretched out on the couch with Jack at her feet and took a nap. I sat in the recliner and watched the Christmas movie, *A Christmas Carol*.

I felt good about my coming marriage. We had yet to set a date, but that would be decided in time. We were right together. The thought of Miriam crept into my mind. I would pray for her happiness.

"Thanks, God; I owe you one," I said quietly as I watched Tina sleep.

Chapter Sixteen

I T WAS THE MIDDLE OF JANUARY when I got the news. I called Mom to see how they were doing and let them know Tina and I were engaged to be married.

"That's wonderful news," Mom said. "Your father and I are so happy for both of you."

"How are Connie and the baby doing?" I asked.

"Connie and your little niece Patty are doing fine. Her divorce from Tim is final now. She is living with her parents and working as a secretary at the gas company," Mom said with a sigh.

"How is Tim doing?" I asked.

After a slight hesitation, Mom said, "Tim is in the hospital with a broken leg. He was driving drunk and slammed into a tree. This is his third drunk driving charge, so when he gets out of the hospital, he will go to court and then probably to jail."

"Look at it this way, Mom," I said, "it might be the only way to dry him out and get him back on track."

"That's what your father is hoping will happen," Mom said. "It's just so sad that this could be the solution to his problem."

I told Mom we would let her know when the actual marriage date was and said goodbye.

Tina was all excited when she got home Friday afternoon.

"*The Journal Star* in Lincoln is going to buy the weekly paper here in town and make it a daily paper," she said in a rush. "My editor asked me if I would be the assistant editor."

"Who will be the editor?" I asked her.

"They hired a guy from Omaha who won the Editor of the Year award for Nebraska this year," she said.

"When is all this going to happen?" I asked her.

"The attorneys are working on the fine print right now, so by the end of February I will be moving back here for good!" she said with a big smile.

"Is this the same reporter who wanted to go to Chicago or New York?" I asked with a grin.

Tina grabbed me in a bear hug and said, "I know now that this is what I want to do. I want to work at this paper in this town with this guy as my husband."

To celebrate the news, we went to Mom's Diner for supper. Sally was working, and Tina told her the news.

"I think that's wonderful, as long as it doesn't interfere with my wedding in May," she said with a laugh.

Tina was to be Sally's maid of honor. They had been making plans, with Cora's help, for the last month.

By the first week in March, we finished the last house Pete had contracted to build after the tornado. The site we had been working on when the twister went through was ready to be rebuilt. The bulldozers, backhoes and dump trucks had done a good job cleaning up all the debris and clearing the downed trees. The power had been restored, and the inspectors had given their go-ahead.

The town was growing to the west and south, and some new businesses had set up shop. The newspaper was now a daily paper bringing us news from across the state and the nation. Tina had put in some long hours making this happen, and her paychecks made mine look paltry. I loved every minute of it. She was in her element, and her new boss was smart enough to let her call her own shots. Jack wore off some of his extra weight just trying to keep up with her.

The Catholic church had lost part of the steeple on the church. A contractor from Omaha who specialized in this kind of work was called in to do repairs. The bishop of the local diocese had also put in a request to build a Catholic school. This would work its way up the chain and be decided by the guys in red hats. The way the town was growing, it looked like it could happen.

There was a mall being talked about by the City Council, but this would come up for a vote at election time. The new mayor seemed like a good businessman, and it helped that his wife was his new secretary. No hanky-panky here, folks! Main Street would get new stop lights in June, and the courthouse would get a facelift at the same time.

When I first started laying block with Henry, I had joined the local Union. With Henry's approva,l the Union certified me as a mason. I still needed to work more with brick, but this was a big step in my career. I now worked on my own, and Pete was happy to have another block-layer. We had a deal that I would work for him for a full year after being certified. The way Pete and I got along, I probably would stick around longer than that. An honest contractor is what every worker hopes to labor for, and Pete was at the top of the chain.

It was April, and the temperature was already climbing to the high seventies. This morning when I was leaving for work, Jack was waiting by the truck. Tina came out of the house with my thermos, gave me a kiss and said, "You boys have a good time today."

I opened the door, and Jack jumped in. I guess he had gotten tired of following Tina around the office and wanted some fresh air today.

We got to the worksite at seven, and Jack went exploring in the new grass to the west of the building. By eight o'clock, I took a break to move my line up. I heard Jack barking but didn't pay too much attention. Sometimes he got on a rabbit track and barked to let me know. This time the barking became steady and louder.

Thinking maybe something was wrong, I went to check. A man was on the ground dragging himself along using his right leg and right arm. The left leg was bleeding below the knee, and he held a pistol in his left hand.

"Down, Jack," I said, and he quit barking.

"Get over here and give me a hand," the man snarled.

I started backing up slowly, and Jack followed.

BANG!

The man fired the pistol once in the air, then pointed it at me.

"You got a car?" he said, trying to sit up.

"I've got a truck parked over there," I said as I pointed toward the house.

"You help me to get over there, or I'll shoot the dog," he said, trying to stand.

"Take it easy, mister. I'll help you," I said as I bent down to get my arm around his shoulders.

As we walked slowly toward the truck, I could see the crew in the shell of the house watching us.

"All of you stay in the house," the man shouted. "I'll shoot the first one who steps out!"

I got him to the truck and held him as I opened the door. As he turned to face me, Henry rose up from the truck bed and swatted him on the side of the head with a crowbar!

The man dropped like a dead weight and lay still. I picked up the pistol and looked at Henry.

"When I saw him wave that gun around, I was pretty sure this was where you were headed, so I laid down in the truck and waited for you," Henry said with a satisfied smile.

We tied the man's hands and feet with chalk line and laid him in the truck bed. Jack, Henry and I drove to the police station, and Henry went inside while I waited by the truck.

The man was just coming around when six policemen came running out of the station waving guns.

I stepped back with my hands in the air and said, "He's in the back of the truck, and he is all yours."

Someone inside had called the ambulance which rolled to a stop on the street right behind me.

One officer cut the line from his hands and feet and clicked on a pair of handcuffs. The police chief came out and told Henry and me we would have to give a statement before we left.

"Who the hell is that guy?" asked Henry scratching his head.

As we were telling the police what happened, Tina came through the door, pushed an officer aside and came running over.

"Are you and Jack okay?" she demanded.

I stood up and softly held her shoulders. "Jack and I are fine, thanks to Henry," I said with a grin.

She turned to see Henry still sitting there, took his face in her hands, kissed him gently on the cheek, saying, "Thank you, Henry."

"As soon as I am done giving my statement I will gladly give you the whole story," I told her.

"When you do, I will give you the story on the guy with the gun," she said.

As it turned out, the guy had tried to rob a payroll delivery in Lincoln that morning. One of the guards shot him in the leg, and he shot the guard, who was still in emergency in Lincoln in critical condition. When the guard in the truck heard the gunfire, he directed the driver to lock everything down. The other guard also returned fire, and the would-be robber fled. His car had run off the road about a half mile from our building site. He was crawling toward my truck when Jack spotted him.

This time, Henry was the hero. He was interviewed by the radio and TV stations and got his picture taken with Jack for the newspaper. I ducked out of the limelight and let those two take the credit.

When asked why he got in the back of the truck and waited for the guy, he said, "I figured it was one way to get a kiss from a pretty girl, and it worked!"

After digging into the background of the robber, the press found out he had escaped from a prison in Idaho over a year ago. There were several banks robbed between Idaho and Nebraska. The description of the robber fit the man now in custody. It looked like he would be headed back to Idaho where a maximum security cell was waiting for him. There was also a reward out from two of the banks totaling $2,000. Henry applied for it, and when the check came, he cashed it and demanded I take half. Not to hurt his feelings, I gave in and took it.

CHAPTER SEVENTEEN

"HURRY UP! We don't want to be late!"
We were getting ready to meet Sally and Andrew at the church. This was their wedding day, and Tina was rushing around like a crazy woman.

Jack hid under the kitchen table so as not to get run over. I had been ready for a half-hour, but Tina never noticed. Jack would be staying home today. I had fenced in the backyard and put in a doggy door. As long as his water and food dishes were full, he was a happy dog.

Tina emerged from the bedroom looking radiant and gorgeous in her maid of honor dress. For a flashing moment, I pictured her in a wedding gown and almost fainted.

"Let's go, let's go," she chanted as she cleared the front door and ran for the truck.

The weather was perfect, and the wedding went off without a hitch. Sally was beautiful in her white gown.

Andrew was handsome and sweating in his tux. Cora was smiling through her happy tears, and David nodded his head.

As Andrew and Sally walked arm in arm out of the church, she smiled and winked at me! It was a wink that said, 'you're next.'

At the reception, Cora was filling a doggy bag for Jack. I would go through it later and take out the sweets. If Cora had her way, Jack would weigh over 100 pounds.

I had bought my first suit for the occasion, and I was still getting used to it. I hadn't worn a tie since the Army, and it felt unnatural to have a knot around my neck.

I kissed the bride and shook hands with the groom. I felt a hand circle through my arm and assumed it was Tina.

"Let's dance, handsome," said a voice I didn't recognize. I looked around to find one of Sally's bridesmaids grinning at me. I think she may have had more champagne than she was used to. Then I felt another hand on my other arm.

"This one is mine, hon; find your own guy."

That voice I knew. Tina pulled me toward her, and I took her in my arms.

"I thought I better rescue you from temptation," she said.

"She never told me her name," I said, "but it certainly fits her."

We danced a slow waltz—the only kind I can dance to—then went to find the bride and groom. Sally was getting ready to throw her bouquet of flowers, and Tina joined the pack of prospective brides. As the flowers went into the air, Temptation charged forward and leaped into the air to catch it. As she turned around to show everyone her catch, she winked at me!

"I am going to have a little talk with that hussy," Tina said with a frown.

I took her face in my hands and kissed her. "You have nothing to worry about my love," I whispered.

That evening, Andrew and Sally left on a very short honeymoon. Cora and David had rented them a weekend cottage on Lake Palmer. Tina and I got home late and got a very cool welcome from Jack.

The next morning was spent cleaning up from the wedding reception. By noon, all was right with the world, so we took Jack on a picnic to the local park. Several couples were there, some with children.

We spread a blanket on the grass and relaxed. The wedding yesterday must have gotten Tina thinking.

"Let's set a wedding date," she said.

As I smiled up at her, I asked, "When did you have in mind?"

With a little frown, she answered," It took almost nine months to get Sally's wedding to come together the way she wanted it. How about a year from June?"

"Why so long?" I wanted to know.

"It will give us time to invite your parents and time to work around my new workload," she said.

"How about the first Saturday next June?" I asked.

"That would be perfect," Tina answered as she threw her arms around me.

"There is one thing I have to know," I said with a serious look.

"What's that?" Tina asked.

"Will Miss Temptation be one of your bridesmaids?" I asked as I held her hand.

"That little hussy is a friend of Sally's, not a friend of mine, and she is not invited," Tina answered as she pushed me down and sat on my chest.

Jack came over and licked my face.

"It may break her heart not to be there," I said sadly.

"If she shows up I will break more than her heart" Tina answered with a wink.

I called Mom on Sunday night to check on her and Dad. They were doing fine, but her prediction about Tim had come true. He was sentenced to two years in jail for his third drunk driving offense.

I told Mom about Tina and I setting a wedding date.

"That's wonderful," she said. "Your father and I will be there. We planned on taking a vacation to visit you, and this will be the perfect vacation."

I told her we had a spare room and they should plan on staying with us.

"We really look forward to meeting Tina's parents. Give me their phone number, please. I want to call and help plan the wedding."

I put Tina on the phone, and she and Mom chatted about flowers, dresses and all the trimmings that go with weddings. Later, she called Cora and told her to expect my mom's call.

Mom's Diner was up for sale. Harold, the man who owned the diner, was a widower. When he was gone, Helen was in charge. Harold had taken a vacation to Miami to visit his sister and her husband. While he was there, he met a widow and fell in love again. He planned to sell the diner and move in with the widow.

He offered Helen the option of buying the diner if she could raise the money. Helen and Brad could come up with $4,500. The bank would loan the money if they could come up with a down payment of $7000.

Pete and I stopped for an iced tea after work one day and made Helen an offer. Pete would loan her $1500, and I would kick in $1000. This would make us silent partners. We both knew Helen had been running the place for the last five years and it was a solid investment all around.

"Both of you will have your money back in two years with interest," Helen promised. I told her there was no hurry. I kind of liked being called on to help a friend. After all, it was Helen who had gotten me the job with Pete in the first place.

Tina was thrilled. "It wouldn't have been right to let it go to a stranger," she said.

The new mayor wanted to put parking meters on Main Street. Every business owner on the street showed up at the next Council meeting and assured the mayor that if one meter were installed, it would be his last term in office. The idea was quickly dropped from the agenda. The stop lights did get installed, and for the first few weeks, the body shop in town did a brisk business.

The old couple who owned the shoe store next to the hardware store retired and left for California. The hardware store bought the building and expanded. The manager of the hardware store retired, and Sally's husband Andrew was now the manager.

One Friday evening at home, the phone rang, and Tina answered. I was sitting on the couch eating a bowl of ice cream. Jack sat next to me, drooling.

Suddenly, Tina screamed!

I jumped up, almost dumping the ice cream on the rug, Jack took off for the kitchen, barking.

I thought Tina had somehow hurt herself! She was still on the phone as she yelled at me "Sally is pregnant! I'm going to be an aunt! Isn't that wonderful?!"

Tina immediately called her mom to talk about a baby shower for Sally. Another tiny life would begin its journey.

If you drove northwest out of town, you would find Barney's Bar. The smart thing to do would be to keep driving. Barney's handled the rough trade. It reminded me of some of the bars just off base at Fort Stewart.

The City Council had tried to shut down Barney's a few times over the years, but the now ex-mayor and Barney managed to keep it open.

One Saturday, about midnight, there was a shooting in the parking lot at Barney's. The victim was in intensive care, and the bouncer who did the shooting was in jail.

The council called an emergency meeting and voted five to two to revoke Barney's license and close the bar. Since the bar was just outside of town, a sheriff's deputy went to serve the closure notice. He was greeted by Barney and two bouncers who tore up the notice and sent the deputy packing.

The sheriff called the state police who sent the Highway Patrol in six cars to serve another notice. They were met with gunfire, which they returned. The fight lasted about an hour. The Highway Patrol shot in some tear gas and smoke grenades. The bar was old and tinder dry, and soon smoke was pouring out of the broken windows. Several men came running out with their hands up and were arrested.

The fire department. was called, but the entire building was now ablaze. The last bouncer emerged from the smoke, dragging Barney by the arms. Both had been shot, but not seriously. The building burned to the ground, and Barney and his crew were taken to jail.

Tina covered the story and the trial, which had a few surprises. Barney struck a deal with the district attorney. For a reduced sentence of ten years and a hefty fine, he handed the DA proof that he had been making regular payments to the ex-mayor that allowed him to stay in business.

"Our ex-mayor was as crooked as a bent nail," Tina said as she was putting the story together.

"Was the bar insured?" I asked Tina.

"It was covered, but most of the money will go to pay the fine and the doctor bills for him and his bouncers," she said with a satisfied smile.

With this new evidence, the ex-mayor was put on trial again. He was found guilty and given an additional five years in prison.

The new mayor and the City Council finally got the word from the Catholic church. The cardinals had approved the building of the Catholic school and an additional wing to house the nuns who would be teaching. It had already been approved by the town, so construction would begin in July.

The new housing that had been spreading to the west of town slowly came to a stop. A town only needs more homes when there are more people moving in. The economy had slowed, and everything slowed with it. Fortunately, many of the older homes on the east side now needed updating. As families grew, rooms were added on and roofs needed new shingles. In some cases, the old one-car free-standing garages were torn down, and two-car garages were added onto houses.

Henry and I were working on a ranch-style brick home. The owner wanted a two-car brick garage added onto his home. As we broke for lunch one hot June afternoon, a long white Cadillac slowly came to a stop out front, and a well-dressed man in his sixties got out and strode over to us. He said his name was Dennis, and he owned one of the old brick homes on what everyone in town called 'money lane.' If your family was wealthy, you lived on that street. Dennis wanted to build a three-car garage onto the back of his three story brick mansion.

"I have been using the old stables, but it will be more convenient for me to have an attached garage," he said. He gave us the address and left.

Pete, Henry and I went to look at the home and give Dennis an estimate.

"I need the brick and a slate roof matched to the house," he said.

Henry told him he could not only match the brick but the mortar as well.

"I assumed mortar was just mortar," Dennis said with a frown.

Henry explained "Older mortar such as yours has seen its share of weathering. It's lighter than new mortar. We can match it by using a lighter mixture of cement, lime and sand."

Dennis was impressed with this and asked when we could start. Pete drew up an estimate which Dennis glanced at and stuck in his pocket. Pete and Henry talked for a minute, and finally, Pete told him, "I can have a crew here to start clearing for a slab on Monday morning."

With a smile, Dennis said, "My neighbors think it can't be done. Let's prove them wrong."

I loved the Fourth of July. It wasn't just the holiday I was so fond of, it was what it meant. Perhaps being an ex-serviceman had something to do with it. Mostly it was the idea of freedom for a nation. Any person could be anything they were willing to work for. We had the freedom to worship as we wished, to think and speak as we wished and to live as we wished. The parades were an expression of our love of country. The fireworks were a remembrance of the battles fought to win the freedom we enjoyed. The rest of the world stood in awe of our power. We were the worlds peacekeeper because we knew how and when to use that power. No other nation on earth enjoyed the freedoms taken for granted in America.

* * *

Tina, Jack and I found a great spot to watch the parade. Veterans from every branch of the military marched together. The local schools had their bands out in force. The mayor rode in a convertible with his wife. Clowns handed out candy and balloons. The Lions club was represented along with the Elks club. Business owners had worked weeks on their floats drawn by tractors. Politicians handed out flyers asking for votes, and the fire department had their complete rolling stock of equipment washed and polished just for this occasion.

The entire spectacle of noise and color ended at the town park where the festivities were already underway. A carnival was set up on the manicured lawn, and the hurdy-gurdy music was blaring from a dozen speakers.

There were food stands, beer stands and an area for homemade crafts. Tina and I headed for the picnic area, where Cora and David were waiting.

"There's my little sweetums!" Cora squealed as Jack ran to meet her.

Not far away were Pete and his wife, Brenda. We set down the cooler and basket we were carrying and took the cold beer David handed us. Sally and Andrew were walking slowly toward us. Sally was in her third month of pregnancy and was loving every minute of it. She said she would work at the diner until her eight month, then take it easy for a while.

Helen and Brad joined us, and even Henry stopped for a chat. This was a day for family, for connecting with friends and enjoying the company of loved ones. This was home.

CHAPTER EIGHTEEN

BY THE MIDDLE OF AUGUST, the entire Midwest was suffering drought conditions. We hadn't had rain since a small storm at the end of June.

Farmers were in danger of losing their crops, and fire wardens were warning against all burning of trash or campfires. Once green lawns were a dusty brown, and the fire department was on constant alert.

Henry and I were finishing up the three-car garage for Dennis. The brick and mortar matched perfectly, and the slate roof was almost complete. Pete had landed two more building contracts for neighbors wanting add-on garages.

We smelled the smoke long before we saw any sign of it. A hot breeze from the southwest carried the acrid odor across the town. The fire chief received the call about two in the afternoon. A farmer had been welding on some broken machinery, and a spark had ignited the weeds next to his machine shed. It spread quickly across the dry grass to the house and barn. In minutes, the blaze was out of control. The firefighters did their best to soak down the surrounding area, but the wind carried burning debris across the road to the wheat field.

Volunteer fire departments from the surrounding counties responded to the call. They managed to keep it controlled enough between two county roads to let it burn clear to the Platte River three miles away.

Only one other farm was in the path of the blaze. The house was saved, but the barn, full of hay, was lost.

Firefighters on the opposite shore of the river waited in hopes the fire would not cross. At one point, it looked like the water was on fire. The heat was intense and the smoke rolled in black and gray clouds behind the flames.

Finally, the fire began to die out as it reached the water. Ash drifted on the river, turning the blue water black. The hissing steam rose and mingled with the smoke. A black, smoking path of destruction over a mile wide scarred the landscape. Thankfully, that night it rained. Not a thunderstorm, but a soft, steady all-night soaker that everyone had been praying for.

No one was killed or injured, the farms, in time, would be rebuilt and insurance covered most of the losses. It was another of life's hard lessons.

Helen had made some changes at Mom's Diner. The old booths had been taken out and replaced with tables. The walls were painted and new flooring installed. The overall look was a big improvement that people liked.

New items were added to the menu. Wednesday night was Mexican food night, and Saturday offered Oriental dining. A daily lunch special drew a good crowd, and of course, the burgers and hot dogs were always a favorite. Tina and I made it to the diner once a week. We would pick different nights to get a variety of Helen's great menu.

One night, after we finished eating, we took a walk to see how construction was progressing on the new Catholic school. The basement was in, and the corners were being set. The old church was brick, and it looked like the masons had found a good match for the school. The two would be separate with an enclosed walkway between. The additional wing to the other side of the church, for the nuns, would be attached directly to the church.

When we got home, the phone was ringing. It was Sally. She and Andrew wanted to invite us to a cookout on Saturday afternoon.

"I already invited Mom and Dad," she said, "and mom insisted I tell you to bring 'sweetums' with you."

Tina laughed, told her we would be there, and hung up the phone. She looked down at Jack sitting on the floor next to her. "Yes, you're invited too, tubby," she said with a giggle, "but next week you go on a doggy diet."

The burned remains of Barney's bar had been removed, and a big 'For Sale' sign had gone up. Barney had no money to pay the taxes, so the county had taken it over and was trying to unload it. A group of developers had made an offer on the property, and the Council met to decide if the money being offered was acceptable.

With no other bidders in sight, the offer was accepted. Being just outside the city limits meant that no city business had a say in what would be built. When the 'For Sale' sign came down, another sign went up. This one said the property would be the site of a shopping mall.

Pete was contacted to ask if he would be interested in helping to build the mall. Pete declined.

"I am not going to help take away business from the downtown," Pete declared. He knew others would be offered the contract, but he was a man of principle and stuck to his decision. A contractor from Lincoln took the job, and the site was being cleared to begin construction.

* * *

"I think this guy is crooked and I intend to prove it," Tina said. She was talking about the used-car salesman Adrian Spencer who was running for a seat on the City Council.

His ads had been in the paper and on TV for the last few months. The amount of money it took to run a political campaign seemed out of line with the income from a used-car lot.

Tina had been digging into Spencer's background, and some unsettling things had come to light. He had owed back taxes for several years that had suddenly been cleared up in February. A sizeable amount of cash had been deposited in his bank account, and he had recently hosted a party for three businessmen from Omaha.

After Tina's first story ran in the paper, she started getting threatening phone calls telling her to back off or else. After the second story, her car was vandalized in the newspaper parking lot. A local television station arrived, and that story ran on TV for two days.

When Spencer was interviewed, he denied all knowledge of the damage to Tina's car and insisted she had done it herself to sell papers.

The paper's home office in Lincoln quietly sent a private investigator named Baxter to check on Spencer. It took Baxter only three days to uncover the truth. Spencer was selling cars stolen in other states. They were fitted with new VIN numbers, repainted and sitting on Spencer's lot. He was arrested and was awaiting trial in the county jail. He quickly gave up the names of his suppliers in Omaha. Two were arrested, and one was on the run, possibly to Mexico.

I was doing more and more work with brick. Henry was a stickler for perfection, and it showed in his work.

Occasionally, we did run into a problem. Pete had contracted to build an add-on brick garage to a brick ranch home owned by Alfred. The slab was poured, and the brick had been delivered. Henry and I arrived on Monday morning, ready to begin work. Alfred was waiting for us.

"This is the wrong brick," Alfred declared.

The size, color and texture matched perfectly.

"Show me what is wrong," Henry said with a smile.

"The color is all wrong," Alfred declared.

Henry turned, gave me a wink, and stooped down as if to check the brick.

"I will take care of it immediately," said Henry.

We drove back to the trailer office and told Pete what happened.

"What do we do now?" asked Pete. Henry got on the phone to the brick supplier, who he had worked with for years. He told them to pick up the brick they had delivered, take it back to the yard and leave it on the trucks.

"I want that same brick delivered to the same address tomorrow morning," he said.

The supplier did just as Henry asked. The next morning, we arrived to see Alfred directing the unloading.

"Thanks to me, we now have the right brick," he told Henry.

Alfred was there every day with a different problem only he could solve. I could not believe the patience Henry showed with this behavior.

When I asked him, "Why are you giving in to his every demand?" Henry answered, "It will all be clear to you on the completion of the job."

With Alfred's 'help' it took us a week longer than necessary to finish. On the last day, Henry and Alfred surveyed the job.

"Thanks to your special insight into the problems you helped solve, I believe it looks very good," said Henry.

"Thanks to me, it is exactly what I wanted,"Alfred said with a satisfied smirk.

The bill was increased ten percent to cover the cost of the re-delivery of brick and the added week of work. Alfred never complained, just paid in full for his 'perfect' job.

In Henry's words, "If your customer has an ego problem, charge him for it."

* * *

Cora, Tina and Helen were having the baby shower for Sally. It must have taken Tina a week to find just the right gift. The party would be at Cora and David's, so David, Andrew, Brad, Jack and I were on our own for an entire afternoon.

We decided to spend the time at Palmer lake. We rented a small pontoon boat at the marina and set out to tour the lake and do a little fishing.

The girls had packed us a basket of sandwiches and snacks. None of us were big drinkers, so root beer was the choice for all of us. Brad was the real fisherman among us, so he was the pilot.

It was about ten degrees cooler on the water, which felt great on an eighty-five-degree day.

"It must be wonderful to own a home on a lake," Andrew said with a sigh.

"It is wonderful until you get the property tax bill," David said with a grin.

The houses and perfectly kept lawns did look great, but the upkeep must have cost plenty.

Brad was casting for northern pike, but no hits so far.

"Have you and Sally settled on a name for the baby?" I asked Andrew.

"She has a list of names she took to the shower. She is hoping for a few more ideas," Andrew said.

A big power boat pulling a water skier blew past us. The guy behind the wheel was steering with one hand and chugging a beer with the other. The wake rocked us some, then settled down.

We cruised the lake for about two hours, stopping now and then to give Brad a chance to fish. He hooked a small pike that gave a good fight, but Brad finally landed it and let it go.

We found a shady spot where a tree hung out over the river and tied up for lunch. As we ate, the power boat came by again at full speed, this time a girl was water skiing, and she waved at us.

Two old timers in a twelve-foot aluminum with a twelve-horse Mercury engine cruised by, one on the motor and one casting. We untied and slowly headed back to the marina.

Being on the water for a day was relaxing, and I made a mental note to get Tina out here some Sunday afternoon.

About that time, we heard the crash.

WHUMP! SCREECH!

We swung out from the shore a little and saw the power boat half out of the water, hung up on a deadhead log laying just under the water not far from shore. The girl skier was all right, just floating in the lake in her life vest.

We picked her up first, then motored closer to check on the two guys in the speed boat. The driver had a little blood trickling from a big knot on his forehead where he had hit the steering wheel. The other guy just looked dazed but otherwise unhurt.

We loaded them into our boat, and soon we were back at the marina. We dropped them off to explain the accident and turned in the keys to the pontoon boat at the office.

"Did you see what happened?" the marina manager asked us.

We all shook our heads no, and I explained, "We got there after it happened, so we just picked them up and dropped them off here."

When we got to the car, we all agreed the driver was probably drunk, but that was his problem, not ours.

CHAPTER NINETEEN

TOWARD THE END OF OCTOBER, the work began to slow down for the coming winter. It looked as if I might be taking some time off for a few months. Henry and I had a few small jobs to complete. A chimney repair and a pair of new windows in a brick ranch would done in no time.

As we were finishing up the chimney, a black Cadillac drove up and parked behind my truck. Two men stepped out and looked up to where we were working. Henry climbed down the ladder and talked to them for about fifteen minutes. The two men got back in the car and drove away. Henry climbed back up with a big smile on his face.

"Those guys were from the church," he said, "and they need two more masons to finish their school and nuns' house by the end of the year."

"When do we start?" was my only question.

"We will be done with this by Friday, so I told them we would be there Monday morning," Henry said.

This was good news. It would take us through the holidays, which was important to both of us.

Tina and I went to church Sunday morning with her parents. The service was upbeat with the coming holidays. The weather was turning cooler and the mornings sometimes showed ground frost. The sermon was on helping the poor.

There were a few families in town who were not too well off. The churches helped them with food and donated goods. How they repaid the generosity of their fellow man was another matter.

After the Mass was over, we were invited to Sally and Andrew's for brunch. Sally made the most wonderful coffee cake I ever tasted. As we left, Cora pressed a napkin-wrapped bundle into my hands.

"Just a little something for my sweetums," she said with a wink.

When I opened it to look, it was a frosted sweet roll as big as my fist. I smiled and thanked Cora. Jack would get the part that I didn't eat.

That afternoon, Tina and I worked on things we needed for the wedding. The list kept getting longer and longer, and I wondered about the cost, but when I looked into Tina's shining eyes, all I could see was happiness.

We completed work at the church five days before Christmas. There was still some drywall to be taped and painted and some light fixtures to be installed, but our work was done. Henry and I got a bonus for helping to get the job finished ahead of schedule.

When I got home that afternoon, Tina said, "Helen called and wants us to come to their Christmas party at the diner tomorrow night."

"We go, but Jack stays home," I answered.

Jack whined and slunk into the bedroom.

"He understands what you said," Tina replied with a giggle.

"It is hell living with a dog who is smart and spoiled," I said with a sigh.

Tina opened the oven, and the delicious odor of her meatloaf wafted through the house. Jack followed his nose back to the kitchen with his tail up and wagging. As we sat down to eat, I told Tina about the bonus.

"That will help toward the wedding," she said between bites.

"If we elope tonight we could spend it on a treadmill for Jack," I replied with a wink.

A little meatloaf mixed with his food made Jack a happy dog the rest of the evening.

The party at Mom's Diner was served buffet-style. All the regular customers were there. Christmas garland decorated the walls, and a small tree shone brightly in one corner. A large punch bowl held homemade eggnog, and two large urns dispensed hot apple cider and coffee. Two tables end to end groaned under the weight of ham, fried chicken, bowls of mashed potatoes, several different kinds of salads, bread, rolls and a half dozen types of dessert.

Pete and his wife Brenda were at a table by the wall, and Tina and I joined them.

"I have some small indoor jobs lined up for January if you are interested," Pete said with a grin.

"Anything to help pay for the wedding is welcome," I said.

"Quiet, everybody!" Helen shouted above the noise.

The talk slowly died down, and Helen made a little speech. "I want to thank all of you for showing up tonight," she said, "and I have a special thank you to the two people who helped make this possible."

With that, she handed Pete and I each an envelope. "Would you open them please?" she asked us.

Pete went first, and inside was a check for $1,800. Pete's original investment, plus interest. I opened mine, and there was a check for $1,200.

My investment plus interest. "Are you sure you can afford to do this now?" Pete asked.

"I can afford this and the party and still have plenty left over," Helen said as she gave Pete a hug.

The crowd broke into applause, and we headed for the food tables. I was about to take some ham for Jack when I saw Tina slip a napkin-wrapped bundle into her purse. Jack would eat well tomorrow.

Christmas for Tina and me was a budget affair. We agreed on two gifts apiece. She got the new fluffy bathrobe and slippers she wanted, and I got thermal underwear and jumper cables. Jack got a chew bone and a squeaky toy. We were together, and that would have been gift enough for me.

We spent the afternoon at Cora and David's where Tina got a flannel nightgown, and I got slippers. Jack got another chew bone so big it must have taken the hide of a large cow to make.

After a dinner of ham and scalloped potatoes, David and I watched a movie, while Tina and Cora went over wedding plans.

From the kitchen, I could hear Tina telling Cora, "No Mom, we are not going to hire an orchestra for the reception."

I smiled, and David just shook his head. Tina did agree to let Cora order the flowers. She did not agree to a tiny tux for Jack. My dad had agreed to be my best man and Sally would be Tina's maid of honor. Our wedding was six months away, and the plans were becoming solid.

January in Nebraska is a good time to be working inside. We were remodeling the kitchen and bathrooms in an old 1900-style Victorian house on money lane. The place was well kept-up, and the owners were a retired couple from Omaha named Kestler.

The wife had been born and raised here in town and wanted to get back to her roots. We had the kitchen done and were waiting for the installation of the new plumbing to finish it up.

Meanwhile, we had started on the upstairs bathroom. The old claw-foot tub would be going, and a walk-in bath and shower would be built in. A step-up frame had been built around the tub for easier access. The plumbing had been unhooked, and Pete and I were taking the wooden frame apart. As we cleared away the debris and got ready to move the tub, Pete looked underneath for any obstacles.

"What the hell is this?" I heard Pete exclaim.

He reached his arm under the old tub and pulled out a metal box. It was a foot wide by a foot long and about six inches deep. There was no lock, just a snap hasp.

"I wonder why someone would hide a box like this under a bathtub?" Pete said with a puzzled frown on his face.

"Do you think we should open it?" I asked.

"The owners are in Florida and won't be back until the end of the month, so I think it would be wise to open it now," Pete said.

He popped the latch, and the hinge gave a rusty squeak as the lid slowly opened.

The first thing we saw was the pistol. It was a Colt Model 1903 .32 caliber semi-automatic. It's blue-black finish seemed untouched by age. The clip was inside the handle. Taking out his handkerchief, Pete wrapped it around the barrel, carefully lifted it out and laid it aside.

An old *Lincoln Journal* newspaper dated March 7, 1928, was next. I lifted out the paper and unfolded it. The headline read, 'Socialite Murdered in Lincoln,' with a picture of a woman neither of us recognized. Under the newspaper was a layer of banded one hundred dollar bills!

"There must be thousands of dollars here," Pete said as we both stared at the money.

"I think we better call the police," I told Pete.

"I think you're right," he said. "This is more than we signed on for."

We carefully laid everything back in the box just as we had found it and carried it downstairs to use the phone in the kitchen.

Police Chief Carl Finch showed up about fifteen minutes later. He met us in the kitchen, and we told him how we had found the box.

"Did you touch anything?" was his first question.

Pete explained how he had taken out the pistol and I had opened the paper. Without opening the box, Chief Finch tucked it under his arm and said, "I'm taking this back to the station for safekeeping. We will dust the gun for prints and check the serial number to find out who may have owned it. I'll let you know what we find."

As soon as he left, I got on the phone to Tina at the newspaper and gave her the story.

"I can do some checking here and find out who owned the house then," she said.

The rest of the afternoon, Pete and I threw ideas back and forth about what might have happened. 1928 was right in the middle of the prohibition era. It was a time of gangsters, flappers and bank robbers. We were counting on Tina to dig up the story behind the box. We were not counting on the police to be forthcoming with any details.

After work, I stopped at the newspaper office where Tina had her desk covered with maps, deeds and title transfers.

"The house was owned by Taylor and Eunice Malone," she said. "She was from a rich Omaha family, and he was a banker's son. They were married in 1921 and had the house built in 1923."

"Did you find a copy of that old newspaper?" I asked her.

"I called the newspaper office in Lincoln," she said, "and they are sending me a copy of the paper from that day."

"Have you talked to the police yet about the gun and the money?" I asked.

With an exasperated sigh, Tina said, "The only thing the police would confirm is that the gun was registered to Taylor Malone."

When I got home, I called Pete to let him know what Tina had found out.

"I remember stories about the Malone family," Pete said, "and the rumor was that Taylor's father, Nelson, was laundering money for the Irish mob out of Chicago."

This was something Tina would be interested in, I thought. This was the kind of story that Tina lived for.

It took Tina a week of digging through back issues of *The Lincoln Journal* to come up with what was still an open murder case. A lot of the information came from the society section of the paper. It seems that The young Malone's had more of a convenient marriage than a loving marriage. Taylor Malone was already in his early forties and considered a ne'er-do well by his family. Eunice was not the most beautiful twenty-two-year-old single daughter of a once-wealthy family. The two were matched up by their fathers in hopes of settling them both down and raising a family. The outcome was unexpected.

Eunice became addicted to the speakeasy lifestyle, while Taylor found himself finally falling in love with her. There were rumors that Eunice was having an affair with the man who delivered the money from Chicago. One night, in March of 1928, as she was leaving a nightclub in Omaha, she was shot twice in the heart by an unknown gunman who fled the scene. Two nights later, Taylor Malone was found shot once in the back of the head at the rear entrance of the same nightclub. The suspect was believed to be the man Eunice was having an affair with. He was never found.

"I believe that Taylor shot Eunice out of jealousy, and then her lover shot Taylor," Tina explained.

The police still were not talking, so Tina and her editor told them they were going to run the story in the Sunday edition of the *Journal*.

"You have to wait until our investigation is done," said the police chief.

"How far have you gotten with your investigation?" Tina asked him.

"No comment," said Chief Finch.

The story ran that Sunday, along with the chief's 'no comment.' Tina had also contacted the Kestlers in Florida who owned the house to fill them in on the story. They returned from Florida that week and immediately went to the police to claim the money found in the box. Police Chief Finch refused to release the money, saying it was evidence.

The Kestlers hired an attorney from Omaha who filed against the police department. for the release of the money stating it was their property, found in their home and not linked to any crime. The judge agreed, and the money was released. When it was finally counted, it totaled $25,000. The police did keep the pistol, the newspaper and the box.

Tina received an award from the Newspaper Association for her investigation. Pete and I were each given a $1000 reward for turning in the money. We finished the remodeling in February and took some well-deserved time off.

/ CHAPTER TWENTY

A NDREW WAS A walking wreck. Tina and I met
him at the hospital as they were wheeling Sally
into the delivery room. The labor pains had
started that morning, and Andrew had
immediately taken her to the emergency room.

As we were trying to calm him down, David and Cora
arrived. To my amazement, I saw a different Cora emerge.
She smiled and took Andrew's hand and sat him down.

"There is nothing to worry about, dear," she said
calmly as she looked into his eyes. "Sally is a strong,
healthy woman and will deliver you a strong, healthy
baby. Have you chosen a name yet?"

Andrew grinned and said, "If it's a girl we will call her
Angela, and if it's a boy he will be Robert."

"That's wonderful, dear. Now relax, and I will get us
some coffee."

Tina winked at me and said softly, "Mom is a lot
tougher than people think. In a crisis, she is the one who
can hold it together."

David was calmly relaxing and reading the paper he had bought with him. Cora returned carrying a small tray with cups and a jug of coffee.

"The ladies in the cafeteria are wonderful. They sent this with me, and they are bringing us some fresh pastries."

It seemed like forever, but three hours later, the doctor came out of the delivery room, smiling.

"Andrew, would you like to say hello to your son?" he asked.

Andrew disappeared through the double doors, and Cora asked, "How is the new mother doing?"

"She is doing terrific. It was one of the easiest births I've done this year," the doctor said.

Just then, Andrew came out carrying a squalling blanket-wrapped bundle. There were tears in his eyes and a smile on his face.

"Everyone, meet my son, Robert," he said in a hushed tone.

As we gathered around to see this new life, the doctor said, "Give us a half-hour to get the new mother presentable, then you all can join her."

Cora gently removed her new grandson from his father's arms and pressed him softly to her breast as she gently rocked him with her arms. The baby quieted down and slowly moved his little fists in circles as he stared up at his grandmother.

David had his camera with him and was busy snapping pictures. Cora handed the baby to Tina who had been waiting to hold him. She looked at me with a small tear at the corner of each eye.

"Someday soon," I said softly.

Tina nodded her head and understood.

A nurse walked up and said, "Sally is asking for all of you. You can go in now."

We walked through the double doors, and almost reluctantly, Tina handed the baby to Sally. The smile on Sally's face put the sun to shame.

"Isn't he beautiful?" she said with a motherly sigh.

"Other than you and Tina, he is the most beautiful baby I have ever seen," Cora said with a little laugh.

David took a picture of Sally, Andrew and Robert, which he would later have blown up to an 8 x 10 print suitable for framing.

* * *

Blain Whitney was inmate number 21538, serving a life sentence for murdering his ex-wife and her mother. Whitney had been a model prisoner working in the laundry area of the state prison in Lincoln.

For twenty years, he had been friendly to guards and other prisoners. He was a regular at the prison library and even took classes to obtain his GED. Then, one morning when the laundry truck from Omaha had pulled in to unload, Whitney had knocked the driver out with a wooden mallet, tied and gagged him and changed into the driver's uniform. He then drove quietly out of the service gate and drove to Omaha where he left the truck parked on the street and disappeared.

The entire state was in an uproar, demanding the immediate capture of Mr. Whitney. The governor's office was getting hundreds of calls daily wondering what progress was being made to recapture this escaped murderer.

Tina sensed a story behind the escape of Whitney and began doing some research into the background of him and his family.

"The original story of the murder mentioned that when Whitney's wife got their divorce, she was six months pregnant with their child. When she was killed, she had already delivered the child, a baby girl. What happened to the baby?" she asked.

"Does the story mention any other family members?" I asked Tina.

"The wife's father was dead," Tina said, "but she had a half-sister, Beverly Martel, who lived in Blue Hill, about an hour's drive from Lincoln."

Tina was making notes on a tablet when she said, "What I have to do is look at the trial transcript and find out why Whitney killed his wife and her mother."

The manhunt was widening its search to surrounding states. So far, no sign of Whitney had been found.

At noon, I drove to the newspaper office to check on Tina's progress in her search. She had the transcript of the trial spread out on her desk and was on the phone when I walked in. As she hung up the phone, she was making notes.

She looked up with a big grin on her face and said, "I got a copy of the police report from the day of the murder. Whitney killed his wife and her mother because of a custody fight over the baby. They refused to tell him where the child was, and in a rage, he shot them both. The neighbors heard the shouting during the argument and called the police. They arrived at the house as Whitney was running out the door, and took him into custody."

"Was there any mention of the baby at the trial?" I asked.

"The court appointed a lawyer for Whitney, but he refused to talk to the lawyer or anyone else. The lawyer never mentioned the baby because he never knew about it," Tina answered.

I thought for a minute and said, "Let's take a drive over to Blue Hill and see if we can find Beverly."

"I love the way you think," Tina said as she grabbed her coat and purse.

Beverly Martel was no longer listed in the phone book. Blue Hill did have a weekly paper, and we spent about an hour looking for her name. Tina found it under marriage licenses issued over ten years ago. Her last name now was Beecher, and she still lived in town. We got the address and drove to it.

It was a small ranch home on the south end of town, and it looked like no one was home. We knocked on the door but got no answer.

An older lady next door poked her head out and said, "There's nobody home, they're all at the church. Her daughter is getting married today."

We had passed the church on the way into town and headed back that way. The parking lot was full of cars, and we could hear the organ music being played.

"That's why he broke out of prison," Tina almost shouted in my ear. "It's not her daughter getting married, it's *his* daughter! Whitney is in that church right now, and we have to call the police!"

"I didn't see a police station in town," I told her.

"Let's stop at the newspaper office and call the county sheriff," Tina said.

It took a little convincing, but the sheriff and a deputy did show up. Tina and I followed their car to the church.

The bride and groom were just emerging from the open doors as we pulled up. Everyone was so busy taking pictures and shaking hands they barely noticed us.

"Let's watch the doors and see if Whitney comes out," said the sheriff. He was holding the wanted poster that had been circulated across the state and was comparing it to male faces in the crowd.

The wedding cars pulled up, and the newlyweds and their families got in. The crowd slowly dispersed as the wedding party drove away. The last man to exit the church was Blain Whitney. He was still wearing the laundry driver's uniform and was smiling. He saw the police car and slowly walked toward it.

The sheriff and the deputy were out of the car with guns drawn. Whitney raised his hands and stopped.

"I had to be here for my daughter's wedding, but I knew the prison would never let me out, so I borrowed the prison truck and got here just in time. I didn't hurt anybody, and I'm ready to go back to prison now."

Whitney was handcuffed and put in the back of the cruiser. The sheriff came over to where Tina and I were watching all this and held out his hand for her to shake.

"Young lady, you just did what the entire state couldn't do. My report will give you all the credit you deserve and more."

Blain Whitney was returned to the prison in Lincoln. The governor held a press conference in which he gave the credit for the apprehension to Tina and *The Lincoln Journal*.

Tina made one request from the governor. She asked if she could interview Whitney and get the story behind the escape. Her request was granted, and a week later she arrived at the prison. She was escorted to a visitor's room and a few minutes later was joined by Whitney. She told him who she was and why she was there.

"You are a very smart lady," Whitney said. "It will be my pleasure to tell you anything you wish to know."

"How did you know your daughter was getting married?" Tina asked.

Interlacing his fingers in front of him, he told her the story. "Before I shot my ex-wife, she told me that my daughter was with her sister in Blue Hill. I was going to go there next, but the police were waiting when I left the house."

"Why didn't you tell your attorney about your daughter?" asked Tina.

"I had done a terrible thing in a fit of rage, and I didn't want my daughter to suffer because of it, so I kept quiet." He stared down at his hands a minute then raised his head and continued. "After I was sent to the prison, I asked to have the weekly paper from Blue Hill delivered. I told them it was my hometown, so the warden said all right. I followed all the stories in the hope that I could keep track of my daughter. I read where Beverly got remarried and where my daughter graduated high school. Then last week, I saw the wedding announcement and knew I had to be there."

"Did you intend to come back?"

With a little grin, Whitney said "I hadn't really made up my mind on that until I saw the police car. I knew then I was going back to prison."

"Does your daughter know you were there?" Tina asked.

"She will when she reads the paper," Whitney replied, "and I hope she understands that I only want the best for her. I don't expect forgiveness or anything else from her. I only wanted to see her happy one time in my life." There were tears in his eyes as he spoke, and Tina decided to end the interview there.

The newspaper got a governor's commendation, and Tina got a Reporter of the Year award for her story. She was asked to speak at a Police Association banquet and tell how she had followed the clues that led to Whitney's capture.

A week after the story ran, the newspaper got a request from the prison to have copies of *The Lincoln Journal-Star* delivered to the prison library.

CHAPTER TWENTY-ONE

PETE GOT THE BIGGEST CONTRACT we ever expected to get. A new bank was coming to town. A block of old businesses on the east end of Main Street had been purchased, and all the buildings were being torn down and hauled away.

Instead of laying a block basement this one would be reinforced poured walls. There are some real specific guidelines to follow when building a bank. The vault area needed support beneath and reinforcement on three sides. Pete bought in some professionals who had done all this before.

As the frame went up, Henry and I would measure and take notes as to materials and extras. Pete would contract for the electricians, plumbers, heating & air conditioning, security-approved doors and windows and a tile professional for the floors. All of the interior design such as tellers' stations and counters would be the responsibility of the bank to provide. It was something new for us, and we were anxious to get started.

This was an election year in Nebraska. The state senators and representatives from each district were out in force. Yard signs sprung up like ugly weeds, and a new candidate was announcing every other day. All the people seeking office were boobs, idiots, draft dodgers, wife beaters and crooks except for the candidate speaking at the time. Outrageous promises were made, and skeletons were dragged out of closets to rattle in people's faces. Family members who were not presently in drug rehabilitation or serving time for drunken driving were cleaned up and put on display for the news media. There was a new scandal every week, and one by one, the office-seekers ranks were thinned out until only those seriously in contention were left standing and those with serious money behind them closing in on the prize.

One such candidate was incumbent State Senator Fenton Price. Senator Price had been in office for two decades, not because he was honest, but because his campaign war chest was the envy of every other candidate, except for Cordelia Bender-Gray.

Cordelia was from old money. Her grandfather, Tyson Bender, had been an Ambassador to Portugal during the Franklin Roosevelt and Harry Truman years. Her father, Alden Bender, was a name to be reckoned with on the Stock Exchange. His real estate holdings covered three states. Cordelia finally got tired of Senator Price's shenanigans in office and wanted to give the people some honest representation.

Senator Price's campaign committee was knee deep in a real dilemma. The Bender family was the nearest that Nebraska had to royalty. They had donated money to build a children's hospital and a veteran's home. Cordelia was on speaking terms with leaders of other nations. You do not pick a fight with this kind of power.

The senator decided to explore Cordelia's early years for any bit of gossip or possible infraction of the law. Cordelia had attended Wellesley College, graduated with honors and returned home, where she met and married Justin Gray. Happily married for twenty-five years, mother of two children and head of the Historical Society of Nebraska—it appeared there were no skeletons in Cordelia's closet.

The only dim ray of hope for the senator was the fact that Cordelia, having never held a job, had never paid an income tax. It wasn't much, but it would have to do. When the political ads first ran in the news media, there was no reaction from Cordelia. In fact, they ignored the ad and continued to run their campaign on what Cordelia planned to accomplish while in office. This seemed to encourage the senator's staff to run more negative ads concentrating on Cordelia's wealth and lack of experience. Pictures were run in all the papers showing lavish parties and extravagant vacations.

This, too, was ignored by Cordelia's campaign committee. They stayed on track with what needed to be done, and how to accomplish it. As election day drew near, the senator's people played their last card. Several pictures were released showing Cordelia drinking champagne at different functions. A rather negative article was written hinting at possible alcohol abuse. These also were never addressed by Cordelia or her staff.

The Sunday before the election, *The Lincoln Journal-Star* ran a short story and two pictures of Senator Fenton Price. The first picture had Fenton smiling and sharing a drink with Fidel Castro in Havana, Cuba. The second picture showed the senator, who was supposedly happily married for twenty years, entering a motel room accompanied by two raven-haired, dark skinned, bare breasted beauties. In one hand he held a bottle of champagne, and his other hand held the pert little posterior of one of the beauties. It seems the senator often enjoyed the company of Fidel, and this friendship was rewarded with female companionship.

Cordelia Bender-Gray won the election by a sixty percent margin. The week following the election, Fenton Price was served with divorce papers and was visited by the federal government who wished to dig deeper into his friendship with Fidel.

In one month, Tina and I would be married. She was a whirlwind of activity. The invitations had gone out a month ago, and Cora was keeping track of the RSVPs. My dad and mom had their travel plans all set and would stay at our house. Sally was in charge of the reception and Helen would cater the food. Jack and I were instructed to stay out of the way unless called on to assist someone.

Jack had made a new friend in Robert, the baby. He would lie quietly while his ears were pulled and his nose pinched. He seemed fascinated by such a small human. Robert returned this fascination with baby noises ranging from cooing to outright laughter.

Our bank account was taking a serious hit, but David was always there with his wallet open and a smile on his face. Since my truck would not make a very good wedding vehicle, Pete and Brenda hired a limo service as their wedding present to us. *The Journal-Star*, as a tribute to the hard work Tina had done, ran a half-page wedding announcement for us. The reception would be at the Union Hall, courtesy of Henry and the Masons' Union local. I was anxious and a little jittery at the same time.

On a Friday afternoon, after work, I stopped by the church and went inside. An empty church can be peaceful and give you the willies at the same time. Every sound is a muffled echo, and every shadow seems to move on its own.

I knelt in a back pew and silently talked to God. I wanted his blessing for the marriage and asked that everything go smoothly. I asked him to look over Miriam since she was his now, and also to look out for my brother Tim. Asking favors from God is kind of a crapshoot because you never know what you will get in return. Still, it never hurts to ask. I thanked him for Tina and also for Jack. Some might call it praying; I preferred to think of it as a one-sided conversation with an old friend.

I made supper that night. Burgers on the grill with dill pickles and potato chips and a cold beer makes a good meal on a Friday night. Tina and I were relaxing in deck chairs and feeding Jack chips while we ate. I told her I had been to the church.

"Did you thank him for finding me?" she asked with a grin.

"I thanked him for a lot of things," I said. "And I am pretty sure you were in there somewhere."

She laughed and poked me in the side with her beer bottle.

"What is left to do for the wedding?" I asked.

She cocked her head to the side as if thinking and answered, "If you remembered to order the tuxedos then everything is done."

"I took care of it Tuesday after work," I replied, "and Jack is not getting one unless your mom ordered one from that doggy clothing store."

"How about decorating the Union Hall for the reception?" Tina asked.

"Andrew and Sally already have the decorations and volunteers to help decorate. I think Miss Temptation is one of the volunteers," I said.

"If that's true, there may be fireworks at our wedding reception," Tina said.

Jack was sitting by her feet and barked. Either he wanted another chip, or he wanted the fireworks.

* * *

Work at the new bank building was proceeding slowly. It seemed like there was a new inspector there every other day. The blueprints were followed religiously, and the framework was checked and double-checked.

Pete had hired some new help for such a big job. One of them was a college kid named Mike who was there for the summer. He was quiet but reliable. Another was the son of one of the carpenters. He was a stocky six-footer named Bobby who could do some heavy lifting and showed up every day on time.

For some unknown reason, Bobby took a dislike to Mike and teased him at every opportunity. Mike took it well and let it slide off his back. This irritated Bobby who was hoping for a reaction. One day, Bobby took it too far and tripped him as we were breaking for lunch. Mike got up, brushed off his pants and looked over at Pete. With a little grin, Pete nodded his head.

Mike turned to Bobby and said, "Let's have it out right here, right now. The first swing is yours."

This kind of set Bobby back on his heels, but he decided he was ready. He took a roundhouse swing at Mike and suddenly found himself on the ground. Blushing a fiery red, he swung again, and once more landed on his back.

"Stand still and fight, you bastard" he yelled.

It seemed like Mike had hardly moved at all, but each time Bobby swung, Mike would grab his arm and toss him to the ground.

146

"It's called karate," Mike said patiently. "It's an ancient form of self-defense originating in Japan hundreds of years ago. I could have done you a severe injury twice now, but there is no reason to."

"Where did you learn to do that?" Bobby asked in wonder.

"I take classes at the college. After work, I'll show you a few moves that might come in handy some day."

It was the end of trouble and the start of a friendship.

CHAPTER TWENTY-TWO

MY MOM AND DAD drove from Wisconsin to Nebraska and arrived two days before the wedding. It was the first time my mom had been out of her home state, and she was giddy with the experience.

Dad and Jack hit it off like they were old friends. Tina and I got them settled in and gave them a tour of the town. We showed them the new bank building I was working on and the additions to the church.

"When does the school open?" Mom asked.

"Classes will start in the fall, Mom," I answered.

"Who will teach the kids?" Dad wondered.

"There are nuns due to arrive in July that are trained teachers," Tina said.

We took them to Mom's Diner to meet Helen and Sally and had lunch. Later, we went to check out the Union Hall. The place had been cleaned, and there were boxes of decorations waiting to be put up.

We drove back home to relax a little. We were all invited to David and Cora's for supper along with Andrew, Sally and the baby.

"I can see why you like this town," Dad said with a smile.

"It's my home now, and I can't imagine living anywhere else," I answered.

The organ music wafted softly through the church as I waited nervously at the altar with my dad and Pete beside me. Everything had come together just as Tina had said it would.

It was our wedding day, and I was anxious to get my first look at my bride in her wedding dress. After a long moment of silence, the organ began piping out the wedding march, and my beautiful bride suddenly emerged in her white gown, trailed by her sister Sally and Pete's wife, Brenda. She looked like an angel delivered to me by heaven. Her dark red hair made the veil perched on top of it appear to be crowning a dark fire. As if in a dream, she slowly approached and stood beside me with a smile adorning her face.

The music slowly died down as the priest stood in front of us to perform the marriage ritual. He gave an opening talk to us about the duties of married couples and the trials we might face as we go forward. Then it was time to vow our love and claim each other as husband and wife.

Opening his Bible, the priest began. "Do you, Hollis Olmstead, take Tina Marie Bascom to be your lawfully wedded wife, to have and to hold, from this day forward, in sickness and health, for richer, for poorer, for better or worse as long as you both shall live?"

Looking directly into Tina's eyes, I replied, "I do."

The priest asked the same of Tina, who answered, "I do."

My dad handed me the rings, and as I slipped the wedding band on Tina's finger, I gave her hand a little squeeze. Tina then put a ring on my finger and gave me that sly wink that she used to express her love to me.

"I now pronounce you man and wife," said the priest. "You may now kiss the bride."

It was a gentle kiss that promised everlasting love. Then the organ began blasting out the notes of happiness and joy. We turned and began our walk down the aisle. My mom and Cora were both holding handkerchiefs to their eyes to catch the tears. Cameras clicked, and flash bulbs popped as people stood to witness our union. The doors to the church opened, and sunshine greeted the newly-married couple.

The rest of the day was a whirlwind of activity. The reception at the Union Hall was started with music from a local band provided by the father of the bride. The bar was open for the guests, and the buffet provided food for everyone. We danced, we drank, we celebrated. The wedding cake had been Dad and Mom's gift to us, and it was beautiful.

The honeymoon would come later when work slowed down for both of us. Jack was a guest of honor and roamed the crowd, accepting bits of food from anyone who offered. Cora had gotten him a black bowtie, that I had to admit looked cute.

As the sun went down and dusk settled over the town, the guests began to take their leave. The stars emerged, and the band started packing up, and what remained of the food was gathered together and taken away.

Dad, Mom, Tina, Jack and I took a last ride in the limo to our house. Mom made a pot of coffee as Tina and I got out of our finery and got comfortable.

When I came out of the bedroom, I saw Dad sitting at one end of the couch drinking coffee. Jack was lying next to him with his head on Dad's lap. Mom sat at the other end, eating a small piece of wedding cake she had bought home.

I got a coffee for myself and sat down in the recliner. Tina followed and took the easy chair next to me. We made small talk about the day and relived the events that had led to this moment. I felt Tina's hand slip into mine as she caressed the ring on my finger. With a small, silent prayer, I thanked God for my good fortune.

The next morning was Sunday, and I awoke to the smell of coffee and bacon. Mom was in the kitchen, making breakfast, while Tina set the table. Looking out the backdoor, I saw Dad and Jack strolling in the yard, stopping to check the flowers Tina had planted.

"Tell your dad breakfast is ready," Mom said, patting me gently on the back.

Dad came in, and we all sat down to eggs, bacon, fried potatoes, toast and coffee.

"Hollis tells me you used to farm," Tina said.

Dad set down his coffee cup and said, "My father, whom Hollis is named after, was a very successful farmer. He and my mother Esther loved the farm life, and when my dad died, I took over the farm. Then the bottom fell out of the crop market, and the price of raw milk dipped down to nothing. Soon we were living hand to mouth."

Dad took a sip of coffee and continued. "My mother's brother, Noah Thorne, bought the farm from us, and I went to work in town."

My mom set down a plate of toast and said, "Many farmers at that time went broke. Noah and his brothers, Daniel and Jacob, owned enough land then to make farming profitable."

We finished eating, then Dad and I did dishes while Mom and Tina got ready for church. That afternoon, Dad and Mom left for the drive back to Wisconsin. I was sad to see them go but glad they had been here for the wedding.

* * *

Senator Cordelia Bender-Gray was coming to town to dedicate the new Catholic school, which would open in September.

The town was putting on a new face for the visit. The flower beds around the courthouse had been given a thorough weeding and watering. The statue of the soldier in the town square was pressure washed to remove all the bird droppings. The cracked window at the police station was replaced, and for the first time in ten years, all the street lights worked.

The newspaper ran several articles on the good work our new senator was doing in office. It seemed every problem had been taken care of, except for Simon Doyle.

Simon had enlisted in the Army right out of high school to fight in WWII. He was a local hero who came home with a steel plate in his head. During the Normandy invasion, Simon had been wounded when a bullet had gone through his helmet, taking out a small piece from the side of his skull. The bright young boy who went to war came home a partially functioning man who had to relearn all the social skills that had been taken from him.

Simon lived at the Bell boarding house on a meager military pension. His single mother had passed on, leaving Simon with no living relatives. Mrs. Bell and her son Alvin looked over Simon. They got him into a routine of showering, dressing himself, eating properly and coming home at night.

During the day, the town took care of Simon. If he wandered into Mom's Diner for lunch, he was fed. If one of the other customers didn't pick up his check, Helen did. If Simon stopped into the Five & Dime store and picked out a new comb, someone was there to pay for it. Simon was looked after by the town he had gone to war for, and most were proud to do it.

The City Council, however, decided that Simon was not one of the people they wanted greeting the new senator. They asked the police chief to lock him up for one day. The chief refused. He, too, was a veteran of the big war and held Simon up as a hero to be admired, not jailed.

The county sheriff had been in Korea and also refused to incarcerate Simon. With no other options, the Council dropped the idea entirely and hoped for the best.

The town had set up a stage with a podium on the lawn directly in front of the new school. Four large speakers flanked the stage, and red, white and blue bunting draped everything.

Senator Bender-Gray arrived that Saturday morning, followed by a convoy of trucks and vans belonging to every television station in the state. The local police and Cordelia's bodyguards formed a protective wall around her as she made her way to the podium. A few selected politicians and city fathers sat in chairs behind her as she adjusted the microphone and began to speak.

About five minutes into her dedication, a small disturbance was noticed at the edge of the crowd. A man had been trying to walk up the steps to the stage when the police grabbed him and began to hustle him away.

Without missing a beat, the senator directed her gaze to the police and said, "Is that my old friend Simon Doyle you have there?"

One of the bodyguards nodded his head to assure her it was indeed Simon.

"Please bring him on stage and give him a chair. Simon Doyle is a war hero, and one of those who fought for our right to have such a gathering as this."

Having no other choice, the police escorted Simon on stage and gently seated him in an empty chair. Simon slowly removed his old Army campaign hat and waved it at the crowd.

The senator completed her speech, thanked everyone for their attendance and turned to Simon. "Would you be so kind as to escort me to my vehicle?" she asked Simon.

He gracefully offered Cordelia his arm, and they left the stage. The senator would be up for election in a few years, and I was sure she just got every vote in the crowd.

CHAPTER TWENTY-THREE

TINA AND I FOUND OUT that married life agreed with us. We spent time planning for our future setting goals for the present.

Our current goal was our own house. We asked the owner of the house we were renting if he would consider selling. He thought it over for a few days and decided he liked the regular income provided by renting and had decided against selling. We told him we would begin looking for a home to buy. Our rental agreement was on a month to month basis, so there was no lease.

On Saturday and Sunday afternoons, we would drive all over town looking for the perfect house to buy. Tina ran a constant check at the newspaper office for any new ads by real estate agencies. Our savings had been depleted somewhat from the wedding, but we still were in good shape for a down payment.

Mom called one evening to let me know that Tim had been released from jail. He was staying with Mom and Dad temporarily until he got a job and his own place.

"Your dad told him that the first drink he took would be his eviction notice," Mom said.

"How are Connie and my little niece Patty doing?" I asked.

"Connie has remarried and moved to another town about thirty miles away. Patty is happy and healthy and growing like a weed. I will send you some pictures as soon as I get the film developed."

I told her Tina and I were looking for a home to buy.

Mom said she and Dad would like to come out and visit again sometime soon.

"You and Dad are always welcome," I told her.

Later, I filled Tina in on my talk with Mom.

"I would love to have them back anytime," said Tina.

One week later, we found the house we were looking for. Saturday afternoon we were checking out ads but didn't see anything we really liked. We were on the east side of town in an area that had been built up after WWII. Most of these houses were hastily built ranch-style homes that needed work.

We were on Center Street which intersected at the lower end of money lane. As we turned the corner, we noticed a man setting a for sale sign into the lawn of a story and a half brick ranch home. We pulled over to the curb and got out.

With a big smile, the man said, "This home just came on the market today. Would you folks like to take a look?"

He introduced himself as Fred and led us up the brick walk to the front door.

"The owner is a widower who is moving to California to be near his son and his family," Fred told us. He opened the door, and we entered one of the finest homes we had seen thus far.

There were hardwood floors throughout the home except the kitchen and bathrooms, which were tile. There were three bedrooms—one downstairs and two upstairs—a living room and dining room. The windows all looked new, and there were ceiling fans in all the main rooms. A full, partially-finished basement held a laundry area and a neatly finished den area. The two-car garage was paneled and had a workbench in the back.

Tina was squeezing my hand so hard I was worried about ever getting the blood flowing there again. When he told us the asking price, I felt a surge of 'we-can-do-this' rush through my head. It was at the top end of what we could afford but still possible.

I walked around the house to check the mortar and looked up at the roof.

"It will need a new roof real soon, and the furnace should be replaced," I told Fred.

"Perhaps the owner could come down a bit to compensate for that," Fred replied.

Tina and I excused ourselves to talk it over.

"This is the house I want," Tina said with a firm tone.

"If the owner will come down three thousand we can do it," I told her.

We rejoined Fred and told him what we had decided.

"Let's go write up an offer and see what the owner has to say," he said with a smile.

We waited for two days to find out if our offer would be accepted. Finally, on Tuesday, we got an answer. Fred contacted Tina at the newspaper office.

"The owner has decided to take your offer," he said. "When could you and Hollis meet me to go over the details?"

Tina told him she would call back in an hour. She drove to the bank building site and ran to where I was moving my line level for the next tier of brick.

"He took our offer," she shouted at me. The smile on her face made the sun seem dim.

Pete came out to see what the noise was, and Tina told him what was happening.

"You two go get this settled before he changes his mind," Pete told us.

We took Tina's car and drove back to her office. She called Fred and set up a meeting for nine o'clock the next morning. Then we drove to the bank to finalize the loan details. There were papers to sign and an inspection to be made by the bank to protect their investment.

We were both dizzy with excitement and anticipation. We would be in hock for twenty-five years, but this was the place we wanted to raise a family in and enjoy growing old together in.

The next day, we met with Fred and the owner. Julius was 67 years old. He was a widower who no longer wanted to live alone. His son and daughter-in-law in California had been after him for over a year to relocate. The deciding factor was the birth of a grandson. Julius made up his mind then to sell and move.

"Fred told me a young couple wanted to buy my house to begin their married life. Now that I have met you, I believe this is the plan God has laid out for all of us."

We shook hands, and Julius left to meet with the bank director. There were a few details to be worked out, but Fred told us we would probably be able to move in by the weekend.

We left the real estate office and drove to David and Cora's. When they heard the news, they were as excited as we were and wanted to drive by and see the house. David drove, and in a few minutes, we were standing on the lawn of our soon-to-be forever home.

Everyone pitched in to help. Pete showed up with his flatbed truck. Sally and Andrew left the baby with Cora and helped load the cars with clothing and bedding. Henry took all he could in his Dodge pickup truck. The dishes and breakables went into David's car.

We started at six in the morning, and by four in the afternoon we were unloading the last load from the flatbed. Tina and Sally set up beds, hung up clothing, put away dishes and generally kept the disorder from becoming chaos.

We took a break for a cold beer and collapsed on the lawn. A van drove up and honked the horn.

"Anybody here feel hungry?" said a familiar voice. It was Helen and Brad. They had bought a big basket of fried chicken and a tub of coleslaw. Tina and Sally spread a blanket on the lawn, and Brad carried a box filled with paper plates and plastic spoons and forks.

We sat cross-legged on the blanket and dug in to the food. Later, Tina took the women on a tour of the house. I could hear their gasps of surprise and excitement through the open windows.

Henry had done his own tour and remarked, "I wish they still built houses like this. It's solid as the day it was built, and not a crack in the mortar anywhere."

Jack did his own inspection and seemed happy with the results. The big backyard offered a small garden area to one side, plenty of flowerbeds and a big maple tree.

As the women came out of the house, they were all smiling, but Tina, with a smudge of dust on her cheek, a rip in her T-shirt and hair tied back in a ragged ponytail, was altogether gorgeous.

I lay on my back, looked straight up and quietly whispered, "Thanks a lot, God."

"Hurry up; if we get there late, all the good stuff will be gone," Tina yelled as she ran from room to room.

Jack and I had been ready for fifteen minutes, so we sat in the kitchen, waiting. Tina rushed into the kitchen just as I stood up and set my cup in the sink.

"Get that cute little butt in the truck, lady, we got things to buy," I said sternly.

"Come on, Jack," she said and was out the door.

We now had a bigger house, which meant we were short some furniture. When you're starting out on a budget, garage sales are a young couple's furniture store.

We found a living room chair that actually matched the couch for ten dollars. A pair of matching end tables for five dollars and a lamp for two dollars at another place. By two in the afternoon, we were winding down and had done well. The last place we stopped at had a bedroom set for sale, and I asked Tina if we should get it.

"No, we don't need another bedroom set," she said firmly.

"But we now have three bedrooms," I said with a frown.

She turned to me with that men-can-be-so-dumb look and said quietly, "We need to keep the other bedroom available for the possibility of having a nursery there."

The look on my face must have said it all because she started giggling and said, "No, I'm not pregnant, but maybe someday soon I will be, and then we will need a room for the baby."

Of course, she was right. Aren't wives always right?

Chapter Twenty-four

AUGUST WAS HOT, but we did get the rain we needed. The crops in the fields were green and growing.

I thought back to the days I had spent working in the cannery in Wisconsin. Had I really been that innocent boy whose whole world revolved around a car and a date? It seemed long ago and far away. Now my world was Tina, Jack and bricks and mortar.

Jack no longer came to work with me. Too much activity and heavy machinery moving around. Sometimes at lunch, I missed his company. He often went to the newspaper office with Tina or spent the day with Cora and David. My time with Jack was when I got home after work. We strolled the neighborhood, making friends and greeting new neighbors.

One of these was Virgil, who was a retired Air Force Tech Sergeant. Virgil and his wife Darlene lived two houses up on Center Street. Their daughter was away at college, and Virgil was working in his garage when we passed by. I could hear his table saw going and stopped to see what he was building. Lined up on his workbench were three half-completed bird houses.

"What do you do with them after you build them?" I asked.

"I go to craft shows and sell them," he answered while scratching Jack behind the ears.

"How much are they?"

"Depending on the size and the style, about five dollars each," he answered.

"Do you have any already finished that you can sell?" I asked.

To the side of the workbench was a large cardboard box with the top open. He reached in and took out a bird house painted red, white and blue.

"I'll buy it. How much is it?" I said as I reached for my wallet.

"Are you a veteran?" he asked me.

"U.S. Army and proud of it," I answered.

With a smile, he handed me the bird house. "First one is free to any veteran," he said.

I thanked him, shook his hand and headed home.

* * *

The weekend had been hot and humid. On Saturday evening, Tina and I decided to attend the early morning Mass at seven o'clock instead of our regular time at ten. It would be a little cooler and more comfortable.

We noticed a lot of people had the same idea and managed to get a pew toward the middle of the church. In the front two rows were all the nuns who would be teaching the children in September. The priest took pity on us and kept the sermon short. The nuns filed up for communion, and I wondered how they could stand the heat wearing those black habits. As each received the host and made their way back to their pew, I saw the flash of a familiar face. It was there, then gone, but I was sure I had seen it!

I must have been shaking a little because Tina took hold of my arm and squeezed as if to ask what was wrong.

Tina and I took our place in line and made our way to the communion rail. As I turned to go back, I tried to spot the face again, but all the nuns had their heads bowed, so I could not be sure.

Later, as we stood outside the church, Tina asked, "What happened to you in there? For a moment you went absolutely white! I was afraid the heat had gotten to you."

I took her hand and looked into her eyes and said, "This may sound silly to you, but I think one of those nuns is Miriam!"

We talked it over for a few minutes as the people filed out of the church and made their way to their cars. We decided the best way to find out was to ask the priest.

As the last of the congregation left, we returned to the church, hoping to catch the priest before he left. We were in luck. As we made our way down the aisle, he was kneeling at the rail praying. As he stood up, he turned and saw us.

With a smile, he approached us and held out his hand. "I'm Father Bennett," he said, "how can I help you?"

"We are Hollis and Tina Olmstead, and we believe one of the nuns is an old friend from Wisconsin," I said in a rather shaky voice. "I have not seen her since she was seventeen, but I am sure I recognized her face this morning."

Thinking for a moment, Father Bennett answered, "The only sister here who might fit that description is Sister Barbara. She joined us recently from Indiana and is the youngest of all the sisters. If you wait a moment, I will ask the Mother Superior if she could meet with you." He left us, and we sat in a front pew to wait.

"What if it is her?" Tina asked.

I took a minute to get my thoughts together and said, "I need to find out. I owe her an apology for my actions. I have to know that she may have forgiven me for being a stupid boy who only thought about his own feelings. Does that make sense to you?'

With a smile, Tina took my hand and said, "Coming from the man I love with all my heart, it makes perfect sense. To care how she feels is only one of the reasons

I married you. We both need to know, if only to bring some closure to a painful part of the past for both of you."

As we talked, the Mother Superior entered and joined us. With a smile, she said, "It seems that God has decided to reunite some old friends. Sister Barbara is indeed your childhood friend Miriam. She also recognized you at Mass this morning. To say she was surprised would be an understatement. After Mass, she came to me with the same story you told father Bennett."

In a halting voice, I said, "If it is possible, I would like to speak with her. I owe her an apology for what happened in our youth."

With a little laugh, Mother Superior replied, "That is almost word for word what Sister Barbara just told me. If you both come back at one o'clock this afternoon, we will meet you and close some old wounds and make some new friends."

Tina made breakfast when we got home, but I was too nervous to eat much. I went out to the backyard with Jack and hung the new birdhouse in the maple tree.

Tina came out with a cup of coffee. "We need more birdhouses," she said. "I want the tree filled with birds. Let's put up a bird feeder where we can see it from the kitchen window."

I nodded my head and stared at the sky. "I've got butterflies in my stomach," I said softly.

Linking her arm through mine, Tina said, "Isn't it strange how life sometimes comes full circle at the right place and the right time? All this is happening now so our lives can move forward with no regrets and no bad feelings."

I kissed the top of her head and said, "Are all redheads so intelligent or is it just you?"

It was five minutes to one as we parked the truck and made our way to the church.

The Mother Superior met us at the church steps and said, "Let's take a walk through the school and have some iced tea in the cafeteria. Sister Barbara will meet us there."

The new school was all ready for the children that would fill the small desks in September. The smell of varnished floors lingered faintly in each room. The sun shining through the windows cast small shadows in the corners.

We entered the cafeteria and heard the sound of ice tinkling in glasses. As we sat down, Miriam emerged from the kitchen carrying a tray with a pitcher of iced tea and four glasses. She set the tray down on the table and looked at me with a shy smile on her face.

I was lost for words. I could only stare at the woman I had known as a girl.

Then she spoke. "Hollis, would you introduce me to this lovely lady whom I believe is your wife?" she said.

I stood awkwardly and in a hoarse voice said, "This is Tina, my wife."

Miriam walked around the table and took Tina's hand. "I am so happy to meet you. I always wondered if Hollis would find the perfect mate, and it appears he has."

The Mother Superior said, "I believe a short hug between old friends would be looked kindly upon by God."

I turned and gently put my arms around Miriam as she encircled me and laid her head against my chest. It was the moment I had feared and prayed for for years. My eyes misted with the tears I tried to hold back. As we parted, I noticed the same mist in Miriam's eyes.

Pulling a handkerchief from her habit, she dabbed at her eyes, then turned to Tina and asked, "Does he still ask those silly questions?"

The Mother Superior left us to talk. Miriam told us how difficult it had been for her to make the decision to dedicate her life to God.

"I knew in my heart I was being called, and knew it would be hard for you to understand. For the pain I caused you, I have prayed every day for your happiness."

"It's me who owes you an apology for thinking only of myself," I said.

Tina had been listening and spoke up. "How did you get the name Sister Barbara?"

Miriam smiled as she answered. "I realized I would be building a whole new life. When I took my vows, I also took the name of the Patron Saint of Builders, Saint Barbara."

I couldn't help myself, I started laughing and said, "This must prove God has a sense of humor. I am a builder. Actually, I am a mason, and we build the best buildings."

Soon, all of us were laughing and telling stories from our past. Tina told Miriam how we met and married. Miriam told us about her schooling to become a teacher and how she had been sent here by the bishop. She asked about my family and how they were doing.

Then Tina asked, "Is it possible for you to have supper with us some night?"

Sister Barbara clapped her hands and said, "If any of the sisters has family in the area they are allowed to visit one night a week. I am sure Mother Superior would see you as family. I will ask her permission and call you."

She walked out with us and said goodbye at the church steps.

I called my mom that night to tell her what had happened.

"Oh my god, I can't believe it," she said about four times.

I told her Sister Barbara would be joining us for supper one night and the meaning of the new name.

"Your dad is really going to get a kick out of all this," she said.

I asked about Tim, and she went quiet for a minute before she told me.

"Tim is in the hospital with a broken leg. A friend of his was driving, but Tim had been drinking. When they release him from the hospital, he will have to go on welfare because your dad won't take him back here."

She asked if we were all settled into the new home, and I told her we were all set.

Later, over a supper of chili and cornbread, Tina wondered what would be a good meal for Miriam.

"How about angel food cake?" I offered.

After staring at me for a minute, Tina left the table. Sometimes, she has no sense of humor.

Chapter Twenty-five

"As soon as we finish this, we will have to have a party on it," Pete said with a big grin. We were building a deck off the back of the house. Nothing fancy, just a place to entertain friends and relax in the evening.

"I will provide the refreshments, and you will be the guest of honor," I joked back at him.

Jack was taking a nap under the maple tree, and Tina was visiting Sally. I loved Saturday afternoons. It was the first of October, and the weather was perfect. The nights were cool and the days warm, usually with a nice breeze, like today.

"We can finish this today and have a cookout tomorrow," I told Pete.

"Hamburgers, chips and a cold beer sounds like a winner to me. Brenda will make us some potato salad if I ask," Pete replied.

"Please ask," I said, "I love her salad."

I went in the kitchen and called Sally. "Tell Tina Pete and I want to have a cookout tomorrow afternoon," I told her.

"Andrew and I will be there, and I will call Mom and Dad," Sally said.

"Bring the baby so Jack doesn't get lonesome," I said with a laugh.

Henry and I worked so well together it was as if we could read each other's mind. Just as Pete and I were putting away the tools and cleaning up, Henry drove up. He got out of his truck with a cold six pack of long necks and handed us each one.

"Deck looks great," he said. "We should have a cookout tomorrow."

Pete and I almost fell over laughing. When I could catch my breath, I said, "The cookout starts at noon, Henry, and you are invited."

When we finished, the deck looked like it had always been there.

Jack woke up when Henry arrived and was begging for his scratch behind the ears. As always, Henry obliged. We sat down, me and my best friends, and enjoyed the company.

* * *

Sister Barbara was due to arrive any minute. It was Wednesday evening, and Tina had decided to make a meatloaf served with green beans and potato wedges.

Jack let out two short barks, which meant company was here. I opened the door, and the smiling face of my childhood friend greeted me.

As she entered, she looked around with wonder.

"Your home is beautiful, Hollis, you have done well with your life," she said.

"I owe my good fortune to God and Tina," I replied.

Jack and Tina gave her a tour of the house while I sat the table. I was pouring the iced tea as they entered the kitchen.

We sat down to a tasty meal and talked about the paths our lives had taken. Sister Barbara left us with a promise to return soon. I helped Tina with the dishes, getting everything put away and cleaned up. After watching the late news on TV, we went to bed.

* * *

The story broke in the early afternoon, while Tina was in the newspaper office. The ex-mayor of our town was killed in a small prison riot.

Earlier in the day, he had been before the prison review board with his application for parole. After the meeting, he was in the chow line for the noon meal. Barney, the ex-owner of Barney's Bar was angered that the ex-mayor was even being considered for parole. Somehow he had gotten hold of a homemade knife and attacked the man as he was sitting down to eat. A stab wound to the throat and one to the chest had proved fatal.

As the stabbing went down, several other prisoners began taking revenge on suspected enemies of their own. The riot lasted about an hour before guards were able to separate the rioters with tear gas and clubs. The ex-mayor was taken to the prison hospital but died on the way. Three other prisoners were injured, and one guard suffered a broken thumb. Barney was placed in isolation and would later be tried and convicted of murder. His ten-year sentence would be extended to life without the possibility of parole.

* * *

As the new bank building went up, inspectors roamed the building site daily. The huge doors for the vault were set in place with the help of a huge crane. It was a sight to see, and the newspaper covered the installation.

The vault itself would be temperature-controlled with monitors inside and out. As an added attraction, this would be the first bank in the area with a drive-up window so people could do their banking without leaving their car.

The roof was steel-beam with reinforced concrete. Some of the new federal regulations on bank structures seemed to be a little over the top, but Pete followed them to the letter. Everyone working on the site took on a sense of pride to be working on this project.

The new mall on the west end of town was almost completed. It really was just a long, low stretch of shops all in a row with a big parking lot.

Tina and I drove out to take a look at it and see what businesses were there. Out of a total of twelve shops available, six were occupied. There was a shoe store, a bookstore, a hair salon, an insurance agency, a travel agency and an auto supply store. The rest of the shops were empty but probably would be taken soon.

"I don't think any of the businesses downtown have anything to worry about," Tina said with a satisfied smile.

"If this idea ever catches on, there may not be any more businesses downtown," I replied.

"Don't worry, sweetie," Tina said, "I can't see people driving this far out to get what is available right on Main Street."

* * *

Henry had been a widower for seven years. His wife of thirty-two years had passed away from cancer, and it had devastated Henry. He hadn't dated anyone in all that time.

Then he met Jane. A widow for three years, Jane too had refrained from dating. Then, one Saturday evening, the Elks Club held a harvest dance at the Union Hall. Most of the town attended including Tina and I. Pete and Brenda were there, also Helen and Brad.

Helen was talking to a lovely lady I was not familiar with, so I asked Tina who she was.

"That's Jane," she said, "She is a longtime friend of Helen's. I am really glad to see her here. Since her husband died, she hasn't been around much."

We walked over, and Tina introduced us. She was probably in her sixties but had held her figure remarkably well. As we were talking, Henry stopped to say hello. Tina introduced Henry to Jane, and as they shook hands, something passed between them that took them both by surprise. Henry quickly moved on but looked over his shoulder as if to make sure Jane was still there.

Jane now had a slight blush to her cheeks and asked me, "How well do you know Henry?"

I explained to her that I worked with Henry every day and that he had taught me the mason trade.

For the next hour, Tina and I watched as the two circled the hall asking about each other. Finally, Henry worked up the nerve and asked Jane to dance. The rest of the night they were almost inseparable. Helen, Tina and Brenda were giggling like school girls at their first dance. Henry was the perfect gentleman, and Jane hung on his every word as they talked. I was watching two lonely people find companionship, and I was happy for both.

Henry had not been much of a church-goer since his wife died, so it was a bit of a surprise to see him walk in Sunday morning with Jane. Tina was so happy she could hardly sit still. I looked over and noticed Brenda and Helen watching them with a smile. After Mass, we all met outside, and I saw Brenda poke Pete in the ribs.

"How would you all like to come over to our house this afternoon for a cookout?" Pete asked.

We all accepted, and the ladies moved off to talk food. Pete and I didn't want to get too personal with Henry, so we talked about work until Henry said, "I have to tell you guys that I haven't been this happy in seven years. I never expected to feel this way again, but I might be falling in love!"

On the way home, Tina and I compared notes. I told her what Henry had said, and she squealed right in my ear!

"Oh my god, Jane said almost the same thing! She said she never expected to meet another man who made her feel like a girl again."

Tina had agreed to make a dessert for the cookout, so I helped her make a chocolate cake. While it was cooling, Jack and I hung up another birdhouse I had bought from Virgil. He said this one was for finches and that was why the hole was smaller. I had noticed several finches at the feeder and liked their bright colors.

"The cake is ready, Hollis; let's go," Tina yelled from the kitchen.

That afternoon, I watched Henry and Jane and learned a lesson about love. They were finding joy in small things like holding a chair or pouring a glass of iced tea. They talked little of the past, enjoyed the present and looked forward to the future. A touching of hands would bring a smile to both faces.

Helen, Brenda and Tina were almost giddy with girlish glee. We all made plans to get together soon.

At home that evening, Tina was in a special mood. As we snuggled on the couch, she said softly, "I want children soon. I want to be a mother to our baby. I watched Henry and Jane today and realized how much I love you and want to have a child that is a part of both of us."

I did not need convincing. I had been thinking the same thing for some time but didn't want to push Tina. I stood up, picked her up in my arms and carried her into the bedroom.

* * *

The phone call from Dad was a surprise, but the news was welcome. He told me that when Tim had been released from the hospital, he had checked into a halfway house, and seemed to retreat within himself. Somewhere in the house, he had picked up a Bible and began reading it. A week later, he went to an AA meeting.

After the meeting, he walked four blocks to the church. What happened in the church is still a mystery because Tim isn't ready to talk about it yet. Whatever it was made Tim decide to go off the booze and put his life in God's hands.

He came home to visit and told our parents he was taking a new direction in his life.

"Your mom and I will give him what help we can, but he is determined to go straight," Dad said.

I told Dad to have him call me when he found the time.

Later, I told Tina what Dad told me.

"If he is as strong as his brother, he should have no problem getting back on track," she said with a wink.

* * *

It was the end of October, and the last of the leaves on the maple tree were rippling in the wind. Saturday, I would rake them up and burn them. Jack would miss them. When he wasn't chasing them, he was sleeping on them.

It was Friday evening, and we were going to Mom's Diner for a fish fry. I was relaxing on the couch with my feet on the coffee table when Tina came in the back door.

She pitched a newspaper into my lap and said, "Read this while I change clothes. I'll be ready in a minute."

I opened the paper and almost had a heart attack! The big headline read "TINA OLMSTEAD IS PREGNANT!"

Underneath the caption was a picture of Tina wearing a huge smile and both forefingers pointing at her tummy!

I jumped off the couch and ran to the bedroom. Tina was standing with her hands on her hips and a big grin on her face. I stood there waving the paper, unable to talk.

"I had the printing department print that headline just for me, and no, it didn't go out in today's paper!"

"Are you really pregnant?' I asked in amazement.

She hugged me, kissed me and told me, "I got the results from the doctor's office today. We are going to have a baby."

"This calls for a celebration," I said. "How about if I take you out for a fish dinner?"

"You're on, Mr. Big Spender, but first I have to call my mom, Sally, Helen, Brenda, Jane and Sister Barbara and tell them the news. You can call your folks tomorrow and tell them."

I wandered back into the living room and collapsed on the couch. Jack jumped up to get his ears scratched, so I asked him, "Are you ready for a baby in the house?"

He stared into my face and barked once. He was ready. I hoped I was.

As I sat on the couch scratching Jack's ears, I thought back on the all the events in my life that had led me here. My journey from boy to man had taught me so many things it was hard to think of it all at once. A lost love had taken me to a new place and a new love. I was happy. I was with new friends and about to begin a new family.

Thanks a lot, God!

CHAPTER TWENTY-SIX

THE GRAY SHADOWS OF DAWN were beginning to take on shape as I let Jack out to do his doggy business. The coffee was beginning to perk, and I could hear Tina in the bathroom.

Her morning sickness was not severe but still sounded like a bad hangover. At three months, she was just beginning to show. To me, it was amazing to watch her grow and still remain the same beautiful woman I had married.

As I let Jack in the kitchen, Tina slowly shuffled in and sagged in a chair at the table.

"Are you hungry, or just coffee for now?" I asked.

"Coffee and maybe some toast," she said softly.

I poured the coffee, popped bread in the toaster, dumped two scoops of dog food out for Jack, and began making sandwiches for my lunch.

Tina would be off to work at the newspaper by nine with Jack, and I was headed to a new building project Pete had lined up.

On the northeast side of town was a three story brick building that had once been a shoe factory. It had closed during the Depression and never reopened. After decades of neglect, it looked ready for the wrecking ball. An insurance company with a very open mind had decided to gut the building and turn it into their home office.

After several inspections and two meetings with the town board, the final plan was put up for bids. Three contractors were chosen to do the work. The only brick mason in town was Galen Fuller, who would do all the brick repairs. Pete and a fellow contractor, Willy Gibbons, would do the remodeling. Henry and I would take care of the concrete work.

"Just look at that beautiful craftsmanship," Henry said with admiration.

He was right. Graceful arches adorned every empty window space. A brick ledge marked each floor, and over the entrance was a double arch.

"I'm glad this piece of history is being saved," I told Henry.

"I'm glad we are working inside," Henry replied.

It was the middle of January with the temperature hovering around the ten-degree mark. We had one seven-inch snowfall on Christmas eve, but nothing since. The forecast said light snow by tomorrow. The roof was on, and heaters warmed the interior of the building. Today, the windows were to be installed, which would help contain the heat.

Pete drove up with the glass company truck right behind him. As he walked up to us, he was smiling and rubbing his gloved hands together.

"Let's help them get these windows inside so they can go back for the next load," he said.

The insurance company had ordered thermopane windows with a stained glass arch. Henry and I put on our gloves and went to work.

Tina's car was already home when I pulled into the garage late that afternoon. As I walked into the house, the aroma of spaghetti sauce took over my nose. Tina was stirring the pot and humming along with the radio. As I stepped up behind her to give her a hug, the kitchen phone rang. It was Pete's wife Brenda, and she was crying.

"Pete has been in an accident," she said between sobs. "Some drunken bum ran a stop sign and hit Pete's truck broadside."

"Where are you now?" I asked.

"I'm at the hospital. They just took Pete into the emergency room! Can you come down here?" she cried.

"I'm on my way."

As I hung up the phone, Tina asked what happened. I told her about Pete. She turned off the stove, shoved the sauce to the back and ran to get her coat.

Brenda was talking to the doctor as Tina and I entered the waiting room. A little out of breath, I asked, "How is he?"

The doctor gave a smile and replied, "I was just telling Brenda that Pete has a dislocated left knee, some broken ribs and a broken left forearm. For some reason, he was still wearing his hard hat, which saved him from a concussion."

"Can we see him?" sniffled Brenda.

"They are taping his ribs and putting a cast on his arm," the doctor said. "As soon as they finish, the nurse will let you know; then you can go in."

Tina hugged Brenda, which let loose more tears. A sheriff's deputy walked in and introduced himself.

"I'm Deputy Simmons. I got to the accident about ten minutes after it happened. How is he?"

When Brenda told him, he slowly shook his head and said, "The guy that hit Pete was falling down drunk and never got a scratch. This was his third drunk driving accident, so he will do an automatic ninety days in the county jail and lose his license for two years."

Pete's truck was probably a total loss he told us and was at the police impound lot.

A nurse with the air of authority strolled up and said with a smile, "You can go in now, but he will have to stay a few days to make sure the cast sets and his knee stays in place."

A very angry looking Pete was sitting up in bed, slowly moving the fingers on his left arm. Brenda gave him hug around his head and kissed his cheek.

He looked at me and growled, "Go get that jerk that hit me and bring him here."

"Can't do it if I wanted to," I said with a grin. "He is sitting in the county jail sobering up." I told him about the automatic jail time and the suspended license. "I'll call the guys and let them know what happened," I told him.

On a chair next to the bed was the folded pile of Pete's clothes with his hard hat sitting on top. I picked it up and saw a dent where it had hit the windshield.

"Good thing you had this on," I told him.

With a puzzled look, Pete replied, "I don't really know why I had that on. I usually never wear it in the truck, but I was in a hurry to get home and just left it on."

Tina patted his cheek and said, "God looks out for those he loves; even hard-headed contractors."

When we got home later, I called Henry, Galen and Willy to give them the news, while Tina made supper. Nothing on the job would change as we planned weeks ahead to stay on schedule.

"I'm going to do an article in the paper on drunk drivers," Tina said between helpings of spaghetti.

"Will the editor go for it?" I asked.

"He will when I show him the statistics over the past three years on the damage done by drunks behind the wheel."

Jack gave a little woof and held up his paw. He loved spaghetti too.

CHAPTER TWENTY-SEVEN

B Y THE END OF MARCH, the old shoe factory was beginning to resemble an office building. All the windows and doors were in, most of the walls were up, electricity was hooked up, and the new elevator was being installed.

Pete was back on the job but not driving yet. Henry and I took turns being his driver. The cast on his forearm was due to come off in two weeks, then his arm would be in a sling for another two weeks.

Brenda was relieved to get him out of the house every morning. "The dummy has been trying to scratch under the cast with a coat hanger," she told me one morning.

"The itching is driving me nuts," Pete complained.

"If you get an infected scratch, the doctor will take that cast off, treat the infection and give you another cast and add a month's time to that one," I told him.

He grumbled but threw the coat hanger away.

When I got home from work late one Thursday evening, the phone was ringing. Setting my lunch pail on the counter, I answered. It was my dad.

"I've got some bad news, Hollis," he said softly. "Your mother had a stroke last night. I rushed her to the hospital, but she didn't make it. She passed away about two o'clock this morning."

My first impulse was to cry, but I held it back. "Are you doing okay?" I asked.

"I'm fine; your brother is with me, and we are making the arrangements for the funeral."

"I'll leave early tomorrow morning," I said.

As I hung up the phone, Tina and Jack walked in from the garage. I told her about Mom.

"I am so sorry," she mumbled as she gave me a soft hug. "She was a sweetie, and I will miss her."

"Can you get time off to go to the funeral?" I asked.

"I'll take as long as we need," she answered with a kiss.

I called Pete and told him I would be off for a few days. He told me not to worry, just drive safely. Tina called her folks and arranged for them to take Jack until we got back.

It took a while to get to sleep that night, with memories running through my head. Finally, I dozed off into a dreamless rest.

Tina and I rolled slowly into Dad's driveway Friday evening. After the hugs and handshakes, we got a good look at each other. Dad was the same, just a little older. Tim was like a different person. He had been sober for a year and a half and had put on about twenty pounds. Dad had got him work at the warehouse unloading trucks.

They both marveled at Tina's pregnancy and wanted to know when the baby was due.

"The doctor says late July, but I hope it's sooner; he's getting active now," she said with a big sigh.

"Might as well keep your coats on, I'm taking us all out for a fish fry," Dad offered.

"Bring some extra money; Tina is eating for about three," I said with a little smile.

Giving me a poke in the ribs, Tina replied, "A well-fed mom means a healthy baby."

The church was packed for the funeral Saturday morning. Mom had been active in the Ladies Aid Society, and the ladies showed up in force. The smell of fresh cut flowers was almost overpowering. There was even a big bouquet from all our friends in Nebraska. At the graveyard, we all wept softly as the casket was slowly lowered into the vault. A reception at the church basement later completed a somber day.

We left Wisconsin early Sunday morning. Dad and Tim promised to come visit us sometime this summer. Tina slept most of the morning, then took over driving through Iowa. A short stop for gas and a bite to eat, then three more hours till we stopped in David and Cora's driveway Sunday evening. A short visit to pick up Jack, and we were home again.

As we got ready for bed, Tina asked, "If this bundle of joy I'm carrying happens to be a girl, could we name her after your mom?"

I hugged her and whispered, "This is only one of the reasons I love you."

That night, I dreamed Mom was sitting at her kitchen table, smiling.

CHAPTER TWENTY-EIGHT

"I'LL MAKE THE CAKE," offered Tina's sister. "We'll have the party right here on Saturday night," Helen added with a smile.

We were planning a one-year anniversary party for Tina. At seven months pregnant, she still went to work every morning for half a day. The other half she spent decorating the spare room as a nursery.

My old girlfriend, Miriam, was a daily caller and sometimes visitor. Tina's mom and sister gave her wanted and unwanted advice on everything from diet to the right shoes.

Her mood swings drove me nuts! She could go from deliriously happy to crying-jag sad in the space of ten minutes.

"He is kicking the hell out of me," she moaned loudly.

I put my hand on her swollen tummy and felt a tiny foot punch my palm. "And through it all, you manage to look gorgeous," I said.

"I do not, I look like a hippo," she pouted.

Jack jumped up on the couch and put his paw on her belly. When the baby kicked again, he leaped back and barked. Caught by surprise, we both laughed.

Saturday evening, I was dressed and waiting on Tina.

"I'm almost ready," she called from the bathroom.

As she waddled into the living room, I smiled and handed her the small jeweler's box I had been holding. With a little gasp of joy, she opened it and took out the bracelet I had picked out a month earlier.

"It's a charm bracelet," I told her. Hanging from one link was a tiny silver dog.

"It's Jack," she squealed.

"I thought you could start with Jack and add a new charm whenever you want to," I said with a grin.

She held out her arm, and I put the bracelet on her wrist.

"I just love it," she whispered. "Now I have something for you."

She walked to the coat closet, opened the door and took a tissue-wrapped package from the shelf. Handing it to me, she said, "This is from me and Jack."

Inside was a pair of leather work gloves. On the back of each glove was a stencil saying, 'My Mason.'

Slipping them on, I realized how rough and chapped my hands were.

"These will protect your hands from those rough concrete blocks," Tina assured me.

"These are just what I needed," I told her.

Giving Jack a scratch behind the ears and a dog biscuit, we left for the party.

The diner was packed when we walked in the door. A big HAPPY ANNIVERSARY sign hung from the ceiling. Two tables were loaded with food and desserts. Blue and pink paper bells hung everywhere. Hugs and handshakes seemed to go on for an hour. Even Sister Barbara was there, dabbing a tissue at her eyes. The town's war hero, Simon Doyle, sat at a table with Henry and Jane. He took off his old campaign hat and waved it at us.

We posed for pictures alone, together and with friends and family. It was a celebration not just for us, but for all those that loved and cared for us. In time, the memories would fade a bit, but the feeling of love and friendship would remain.

* * *

Pete and I were talking and sipping hot coffee Monday morning when Henry drove up and parked. Walking toward us, we both noticed the big smile on his face.

"What makes you so happy on a Monday morning?" Pete asked.

"You guys are the first to know that last night I got engaged! Jane and I are getting married in October!"

Pete and I must have looked pretty silly standing there with our mouths gaping open. Finally, the shock wore off, and we tried to shake his hand at the same time.

"Congratulations!" Pete yelled.

I gripped his shoulder and told him, "This is the best news I've had since Tina told me she was pregnant."

Very seriously, Henry said, "I have a favor to ask both of you. Pete, I would like you to walk Jane down the aisle, and, Hollis, I want you to be my best man."

Of course, we said yes!

"Jane is going to call the women, so be prepared for the news when you get home," Henry told us.

The best way to start a work week is good news from an old friend!

We were outside eating lunch when Tina's sister Sally drove up in a cloud of dust. Leaning out the car window, she yelled, "Hollis, get to the hospital! I just took Tina to the delivery room. The baby is coming!"

I dropped my sandwich and ran for my truck. The hospital was only ten minutes away, but it seemed like an hour drive. I screeched to a stop in the parking lot and ran for the door.

Inside, I ran into Sally, Cora, Brenda, Jane and Helen. With gentle pats and assurances that everything was fine, they guided me to the waiting room. All the questions I had were answered before I could ask them.

"She started having labor pains at work about ten o'clock, so she called me right away," Sally told me.

"I got here with Jane just as Sally and Cora were bringing her in the door," said Brenda.

"I turned the diner over to the cook and drove right over. Now we all have to wait and let God and nature do their work," offered Helen.

Two long, long hours later, the doctor walked into the waiting room with a big smile. "Congratulations, it's a boy," he announced.

Just then, Sister Barbara hurried in. "I wanted to be here sooner, but I had to wait until class was over. How is she?"

"Why don't you ask her?" the doctor said, "She is waiting to see all of you."

Tina was sitting up, holding a small blanket-wrapped bundle. With a big smile, she motioned me closer.

"Hollis Olmstead, the second, meet Hollis Olmstead, the third."

From the blanket emerged two tiny fists and a little scowling face. A fuzz of dark hair crowned the wiggling bundle. Sister Barbara moved to the other side of the bed and leaned down to kiss Tina on the cheek. In that moment, I realized my life had come full circle. My first love had found God, my second love had found me, and a child would bind us together. Mysterious workings indeed!

With a short silent prayer, I again repeated, "Thanks a lot, God!"

T h e   E n d

About the Author

Mark Gengler was born and raised on a small farm north of Medford, Wisconsin. He joined the Army in 1963 and was stationed at Ft. Bragg, N.C. with the 82nd Airborne Division. He saw action in the Dominican Republic in 1965. Upon discharge from active duty, he traveled America, working odd jobs in California, Texas, Colorado, Kansas and Louisiana. He returned to Wisconsin and went to broadcasting school and was a disc-jockey for seven years.

He married and went to work for the University of Wisconsin-Oshkosh. After retiring in 2003, he began to write. His first novel, *Noah Thorne* is published by Christopher Matthews Publishing and is the story of a young boy growing up on a Wisconsin farm in the 1920s as the country was going through major technological and cultural changes.

Sample Chapter

of
Noah Thorne

"HURRY UP, NOAH. We got to get home before the blizzard hits!"

My brothers, Daniel and Jacob, and I were on our way home from school at the crossroads. Daniel was right about the storm coming. The wind was picking up, and a few snowflakes were drifting down. I stuck out my tongue and caught a big flake right on the end. Daniel grabbed my arm to hurry me along. Jacob was already ahead of us and walking fast.

Daniel was twelve and built tall and rangy like Pa. Jacob was ten and took after our Grandpa Cyrus with broad shoulders and a big chest. They both could do a man's work, and often did. At seven years old, I was the youngest of the Thorne kids, and nobody ever let me forget it.

Ours was a fair-sized farm—160 acres with about 100 acres under plow or pasture at any one time. We had two dozen milk cows, some young stock, chickens, ducks, assorted barn cats, our dog Rusty, and a fine pair of matched Belgian horses named Duke and Belle. They were Pa's pride and joy. He had bought them with his mustering-out pay when he got home from the Great War. Pa didn't like to talk about the war much, claiming it wasn't a fit topic for women and children.

As we turned off the road into the yard, we could see Pa had strung a rope from the house to the barn so as not to get lost if the snow got really bad.

"Howdy, boys. I need you all to get right to work," said Pa. "Daniel and Jacob, get the cows milked and fed, and Noah, get the woodbox filled, and stack some extra in the mudroom. This could be a blue norther of a blizzard, and we got to be ready."

"A family of raccoons could live in that woodpile, Noah. Now stack it neat like Pa showed you." My sister, Esther, was fourteen, the oldest of us Thorne kids, and just lived to boss me around. She had graduated from school last spring and helped Ma around the house.

We needed lots of wood to feed the Monarch cook stove in the kitchen and the Buckley stove in the main room. I also stacked lots of kindling in the big basket next to the stove.

Ma turned with a smile and said, "Esther, make sure those kerosene lamps are filled and the wicks are trimmed." Pa ran the farm, but Ma ruled the house.

Just then, the door blew open, and Pa stepped in, shaking off the snow. "Hannah, I need some rags for washing off the cows' udders," said Pa.

Ma was standing at the kitchen table kneading biscuit dough and was speckled with flour. Pa stepped behind her and laid his hand on her waist. "You sure look pretty behind that flour," Pa said with a grin.

Ma turned her head and smiled back. "Esther, fetch your pa some rags from the pantry, and, Eban, if you want supper soon, you better get back to your chores."

Pa chuckled, took the rags, and headed back out into the storm.

The snow was really coming down thick, and the wind was driving it against the windows. It was hard to see the barn from the house. Ma slid a tin of biscuits in the oven and said, "Noah, get your schoolbook out, and study your sums. Esther will help you."

I was in the second grade and was doing good at reading and writing, but numbers were giving me fits.

"If I give you six apples and take back one, how many apples do you have left?" said Esther in her bossy sister voice.

"Four apples," I said with a grin.

"You would have five apples left," said Esther.

"Maybe I ate one when you weren't looking," I said.

"They aren't real, so you can't eat any!" Esther's voice had gone up about two notches, and her eyes were getting that pin-pointy look.

Ma was at the table, kinda shaking her head and trying to hide a smile. "Better set the table, Esther. We will be eating as soon as Pa and the boys come in from the barn. Noah, hang up your coat and cap. You left them on the woodbox in the mudroom."

None of us Thornes was picky eaters, probably because Ma was such a good cook. Tonight, we had stewed rabbit, potatoes, green beans, and biscuits. After Pa said grace, we settled into a fine supper. The wind was howling outside, driving snow against the kitchen window. I felt glad to be inside, all fed and warm with the family.

After supper, Ma and Esther cleared the table, washed the dishes, and scraped the leavings into a bowl for Rusty, our cow dog. In spring, summer and fall Rusty slept under the front porch, but in winter, and especially on a night like this, Ma let him in the house, and he slept on an old blanket in the mudroom.

Rusty was a mutt, born of other mutts, and his main job was fetching the cows for milking time. Pa would yell, "Milking time, Rusty," and Rusty would take off like a shot, clear a three-wire fence with an easy leap, and in no time at all have the cows rounded up and headed for the barn. His other favorite thing was hunting rabbits by himself. He would sniff them out, hunt them down, grab them behind the neck, shake them til they stopped moving and lay them on the front porch. Pa would gut them, skin them, and hang them in the springhouse til Ma was ready to cook or can them.

Pa had settled back in his big chair in the main room and was leafing through the Sears & Roebuck catalog we had got from the store. I was hoping Pa was checking out the gun section. I had been dropping hints to Pa about a .410 Savage shotgun. With Christmas coming soon, I felt I had a fair chance of maybe getting my own firearm. Daniel had gotten a .20-gauge Stevens double barrel three years ago, and Jacob got a single shot Remington .22 last Christmas. I knew I had to be careful pushing Pa about it 'cause if I got to nagging him, he would get his back up, dig in his heels and tell me I was still too young. I figured if I took the long way around the barn and snuck up on it, I could get him thinking on it.

Ma was rocking slowly in her chair and knitting something colorful, probably more socks. Esther and Daniel had a checker game going, and Jacob was lying on the rug, reading a dime novel western he got from Uncle Nathan at the store.

"Pa, tell us about when Great-uncle Silas Thorne came to Wisconsin," I said.

Pa looked up from his catalog and said, "You heard that story a hundred times, Noah. You sure you want to hear it again?"

"Yeah, Pa, tell it again," said Esther.

"Don't forget the part where Grandpa Cyrus was about my age and put meat on the table with his own shotgun," I said.

Pa looked over at Ma, and she nodded her head. He picked up his pipe from the lamp table, packed it slow, and fired it up with a Lucifer match.

"My Grandpa Silas and Grandma Bethel were born, raised and married in Pennsylvania," said Pa. "They came to Wisconsin when this was still a territory. Silas was a blacksmith like your Grandpa Cyrus. He heard about the homestead land being offered, so he packed his belongings and family into a Studebaker wagon and set out. The trip took about two months, traveling through Indiana and Illinois, stopping in Milwaukee to register for 160 acres of land on the Thorneapple River."

Pa took a puff on his pipe, and the smoke curled up around his head like a wispy cloud. The tobacco was Ketchum's Apple-blend, which he got from Ma every Christmas.

"Silas was looking for a place to farm and set up his blacksmith forge," Pa continued, "and he was mighty pleased when he pulled up at the crossroads, right where your Uncle Nathan has the new dry-goods store."

"Tell us about the Indians, Pa," said Jacob.

"Just be patient, son. I'm getting there," said Pa with a grin.

Another gust of wind scattered big snowflakes against the window.

"It was early September when they got here, so the first thing they did was start felling trees and building a cabin for them and a pole shed for the horses and two milk cows they brought along. Grandma Bethel and their daughter, Netta, chinked the logs with a clay-and-moss mix and helped stack the hay the men scythed for winter feed. Game was plentiful then, so they ate well."

Ma got up from her rocker, tweaked the damper on the stove a bit, chucked in another piece of wood, and settled back to her knitting. Esther brought in some apples from the pantry and passed them around. Just when I figured she was nothing but mean, she would turn on me and do something nice.

"The Indians showed up that fall, didn't they, Pa?" said Jacob.

"Yes, they did, son. About the middle of November, Walking-bear and his wife rode in and pitched a tepee across the road where your

Uncle Foley now has his forge. Bethel was a little nervous at first, but Silas took to them right away. Soon, Silas and Walking-bear were hunting and trapping together. Bethel got to know his wife, Willow, and they both learned from each other."

"They were Winnebago Indians, weren't they, Pa?" said Daniel.

"Walking-bear was Winnebago," said Pa, "but Willow was from the Sauk-Fox tribe. She came knocking on Bethel's cabin door one day, carrying her baby in a beautiful woven basket. The baby was wrapped in an old piece of trade-wool blanket that barely covered it. Bethel went to her storage chest and took out a wool blanket that had been Netta's as a baby. She wrapped the baby, whose name was Otter, in that thick, warm blanket and handed him back. Willow felt that blanket over, nodded her head at Bethel, and pushed her woven basket across the table. They had struck a trade!"

Esther let out a big sigh and said, "I just love the part about the baby. It's so wistful." This was Esther's new ladylike word. Every few days, she would spring a new word on us, and it was usually a big one.

I tossed my apple core to Rusty, who caught it in midair and ate it up.

"That's when Grandpa Silas decided to start a trading post, isn't it, Pa?" said Jacob.

The burning wood settled in the stove, throwing sparks up behind the isinglass window. Pa stretched his feet out, crossed his ankles, and relit his pipe. "That's right, Jacob," said Pa. "When Silas got a look at that basket, he knew right then what to do. The next morning, he was at Walking-bear's camp and explained to them what he had in mind. Walking-bear had hung around Fort Winnebago and spoke passable English, but his talk was a bit rough. He told Silas, 'Willow make baskets. We trap. You sell damn stuff!'"

Pa knew he was stepping onto dangerous ground here because Ma didn't allow cussing in the house. Ma looked up from her knitting to find all four of us staring at her.

"Walking-bear wasn't a good Christian, so he didn't know cussing was a mortal sin," said Ma. "Keep going, Eban. The children want to hear the rest."

Pa blew out a little cloud of smoke and continued. "That spring, Silas sent his oldest son, John, to Fort Winnebago with the wagon and what money he could spare to stock up on trade goods and spread the word about the new trading post. Meanwhile, Silas and his other son, Aaron, began felling trees and clearing a spot next to the cabin to build the trading post. By the time John returned, the post was ready. Within a year, the trading post was a going concern. A stagecoach line came through and built a stop across from the post. Walking-bear moved his camp over by the post, and Silas built his forge on that corner. When Silas passed on, Aaron took over the store, and John ran the blacksmith shop and livery stable. Soon, people moved in, took up the good farmland and built a church on the last corner of the crossroads. After the stagecoach line moved on, that building was turned into the school."

The wind was whipping the snow around outside, and I was getting sleepy. Jacob was nodding his head, and Pa let out a yawn. Ma put her knitting back in the basket and stood up.

"Bedtime, children. Lots of shoveling tomorrow. Better get some rest. Daniel, let Rusty out to do his business. Eban, build that fire for the night, and Esther, brush your hair before bed." Ma kissed the top of my head as she passed, but I was too tired to be embarrassed, so I just went to bed.

END OF SAMPLE

Copies of *Noah Thorne* and other excellent books
are available online and at local bookstores
or directly from Christopher Matthews Publishing
http://christophermatthewspub.com

www.ingramcontent.com/pod-product-compliance
Lightning Source LLC
Chambersburg PA
CBHW071301190726
48292CB00007B/2635